I0566030

HIS LOSS

SHINING ARMOR #2

CHARITY PARKERSON

The scanning, uploading, and distributing of this book via the internet or via any other means without the permission of the copyright owner is illegal and punishable by law. Criminal copyright infringement, including infringement without monetary gain, is investigated by the FBI and is punishable by up to 5 years in federal prison and a fine of $250,000. Please purchase only authorized electronic editions, and do not participate in or encourage electronic piracy of copyrighted materials. Brief passages may be quoted for review purposes if credit is given to the copyright holder. Your support of the author's rights is appreciated. Any resemblances to person(s) living or dead, is completely coincidental. All items contained within this novel are products of the author's imagination.

--Warning: This book is intended for readers over the age of 18.

Copyright © 2018 Charity Parkerson
Editor: Hercules Editing & Consultants
All rights reserved.
ISBN: 978-1-946099-29-7

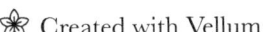 Created with Vellum

There are millions of reasons people could call Richie insane. Richie knows it's only one—losing Bryce.

After an undercover operation went wrong, Richie spent two months in captivity. The experience left him with more issues than he can count. Everything he suffered at the hands of a drug lord is nothing compared to the hell he brought upon himself afterward by leaving the only man he's ever loved —Bryce.

Each morning, Bryce rides the train to work while pretending he doesn't feel his ex's stare on his skin. Richie left him. Bryce shouldn't care how the man feels. He wants to let it go. However, when the pair end up trapped in an elevator, and Richie breaks down, Bryce does the only thing he can think to do to reach Richie. He kisses him.

Bryce's kiss gives Richie something he never thought to have again—hope. Now Richie can't stop trying to win back the man of his dreams before it's too late. He has one trick left up his sleeve that never fails. Richie knows how to set Bryce's body on fire like no one else, and he's not afraid to sink to that level to get what he wants.

TEN MONTHS AGO—JUAREZ, Mexico...

The scent of Bryce's expensive cologne filled Richie's nostrils. The man's sweat-soaked skin pressed against Richie's. With his back against the headboard and Bryce straddling his hips, Richie strained toward release. Bryce gasped for air against his ear. Richie couldn't stop touching the man everywhere he could reach. Two years they'd been together, and fucking Bryce never got old. Bryce was the perfect mixture of sweet and perverted. The man could and would do anything Richie suggested. Even though it didn't seem possible, Richie fell in love with Bryce a little more every day.

Sparks of pleasure danced on his dick. "I love you," Richie whispered, needing Bryce to know. He never wanted him to forget. What if he forgot?

Something was wrong. He didn't feel right. Bryce was slipping away. His palms still felt hot and wet, but empty. The sweet smell of Bryce's cologne disappeared, replaced with sweat, blood, and excrement. Richie's lungs burned as he fought to cling to the man he loved. His pleasure turned to agony. Light slapped him in the face, burning his retinas. He squeezed his eyes shut against the pain. Bryce's loving touch vanished. Rough hands tugged at his body, shouting assaulted his unused eardrums.

Richie's muscles screamed in protest as the rough hands forced his legs to straighten. They collapsed from not being used in countless weeks. His back hit the floor. A scream tore from lips. Still, his eyelids wouldn't lift. The smallest hint of light blinded him. He'd been in the dark too long.

"Agent Tuthill, you're safe. We'll get you home."

Hot tears pressed at the backs of his eyes. Home. That's where Bryce was. Bryce would make him better.

CHAPTER 1

PRESENT DAY—PHOENIX, Arizona...

It took thirty minutes by train to get from the Park and Ride to the Central Crime Divisional building where Richie worked each day. He could drive and make it in half the time, but parking downtown was a nightmare he had no desire to endure. Not to mention, he barely held on to his sanity while on a train where he could move around. In a car, Richie might do anything. Richie had worked for the DEA for over fifteen years. In that time, he'd worked on everything from busting low-level street deals to trying to bring down some of the nastiest of drug lords. That final one was what landed him with four months of medical leave, and sitting behind a desk for the past six months. A year ago, during an undercover sting,

Richie had been exposed as an agent. He'd spent two months living in hell afterward. Now, here he was, taking the train and barely holding his shit together.

There was a second reason Richie chose not to drive now that he rode the pine. Today, that excuse stood inches from Richie, smelling like a million bucks. Normally, Richie kept his distance from his ex, Bryce. He always sat close enough to watch him, but far enough there was zero chance they'd speak. Bryce hated him for all the reasons he should. Richie had come home from those two months fucked up. No matter how hard the man had tried, Bryce couldn't fix Richie. Richie had done the humane thing. He'd left.

The train was busier than usual. At standing room only, Richie had been shuffled closer and closer until there was no distance left between Bryce and him. They held the same rail. Their hands were inches apart. All Richie needed to do was slide his hand down, and they'd touch. The temptation was real and crippling. Richie was hard enough to bend steel. He imagined he was giving everyone nearby a show. It couldn't be helped. Bryce dripped sex. Always had. Richie's body knew exactly what Bryce could do for it. Richie was one step away from completely embarrassing them both. Leaving Bryce had been the biggest mistake of Richie's life. Unfortunately, he didn't know how to fix things between them, so he tortured himself instead. They worked in the same building. Five floors separated them. Richie found every excuse he could to do exactly as he did now—stare and fantasize. He tried mentally willing Bryce to look his way while hoping the man kept his gaze averted. Richie knew he was a mess of mixed emotions. That knowledge didn't change a thing. He couldn't stop. Bryce was gorgeous. He was possibly the sexiest man on the planet. Richie wasn't the only one staring. With jet black hair and light green eyes, Bryce captured everyone's attention. While wearing a dark suit and with his cut jaw covered in a day's growth of dark beard, Bryce was breathtaking. The man had lips that made people want to do naughty things to them. Richie had fucked those lips. Tasted them. He wanted to do so again.

As if Bryce heard Richie's silent plea to look, Bryce turned his head. The sexy green eyes that haunted him landed on Richie. Richie didn't look away. Bryce did. The train came to a sudden stop, forcing Richie even closer.

A chuckle that sounded nervous even to his ears

escaped Richie, covering the moan that had risen in his throat the instant their skin touched. "Well, this is uncomfortable. We're crammed in here today."

Richie's well-dressed obsession turned his head again at the observation. For a split second, their gazes met. The man's mouth lifted in one corner before looking away again. No doubt Bryce thought Richie was completely insane because he couldn't stop staring. It was ridiculous for any one person to be so flawless. The door opened. Bryce stepped out. Richie followed at a slower pace. He didn't want to make Bryce any more uncomfortable than he already had today. It was bad enough he'd been staring at the man like a perv for the past half an hour. When his sexy ex made his way toward the coffee shop inside the high-rise where they worked, Richie almost kept walking. He didn't need his daily coffee that bad. The smell of dark roast permeated the air and whispered Richie was a fool if he thought he could resist its addictiveness. Not to mention, the sexy ass leading the way had him tethered by an invisible chain, dragging him along. Bryce opened the door and held it wide for Richie as if he'd known Richie had been behind him all along.

Richie flashed him a smile as he passed. "Thanks. I promise I'm not stalking you."

Bryce smirked, making Richie's stomach clench with desire. "That's a shame."

Oh, goddamn. Richie's knees weakened at the claim. The words had been so quietly spoken Richie almost missed them, and a small part of his brain—bent on saving him from embarrassment—refused to believe he'd heard them at all. He'd never been more aware of someone standing behind him. Richie fought the urge to turn and talk, pulling any conversation out of his ass, even if it was about the weather. The dude stood so close Richie could smell his cologne—like chocolate and cherries—and feel the heat radiating from his skin. The tiny coffee shop had them packed inside, making their time on the train seem like a luxurious dream. Oxygen felt almost nonexistent. Richie's entire being stayed locked on the man at his back. He struggled to remember what he usually ordered. His thoughts wouldn't steady. Richie's discomfort grew until he found himself turning away, pushing his way through the crowd, and bursting from the shop. He didn't dare meet Bryce's stare as he passed. Richie sucked air like he'd been trapped underwater as he made his way toward the elevator. Yeah, he was still a fucked-up mess. Claustrophobia was just one of the many issues he still battled every second of each day. He stared at the arrows above each elevator door, focusing on nothing while trying to guess which door would open first. Richie tried telling himself he hated crowds. He wasn't having another panic attack. Things were under control. Lying to himself was part of Richie's coping. Healthy or not, the method usually worked for him.

The arrow to his left lit. Richie shuffled closer, waiting for the door to open. Everything seemed to move twice as slow this morning. He hated days like this when he could feel a PTSD attack creeping into his brain, waiting to pounce. Finally, the lift dinged and the door slid open, letting him inside. He pressed the button labeled with a twelve as a second set of shoes joined him.

"Where you headed?" The question died on his lips as he lifted his gaze to a set of light green eyes.

"Seventeen."

Richie pressed the button. His gaze immediately swung back the man's way as the door closed, shutting them inside together. It was the first time they'd been alone in six months. Richie couldn't let the moment pass. "My claim of not stalking you is getting flimsier by the second." Richie kind of wanted to slap himself at the asinine comment.

"Maybe I'm the one pursuing you," Bryce deadpanned. His gaze never wavered from Richie.

He eyed Bryce's empty hands. "You didn't get your coffee." Richie wished he could think of something wittier. Nothing came to mind.

Bryce's eyebrows rose. "Neither did you."

"It was too crowded in there," Richie admitted. "I couldn't take so many people pressing in on me."

Bryce nodded. "Me too."

This was the most they'd spoken since their break-up. Richie wanted to say more. Bryce turned away and focused on the closed doors before Richie could think of anything. He tore his gaze away and focused on the number above the door. It said six. The elevator jerked to a stop. Richie eyed the door, mentally willing it to open. He didn't want to accept what he already knew as the truth. They were stopped between floors. The elevator had malfunctioned. Fuck. Sweat already coated his skin from the coffee shop debacle. He couldn't be trapped.

"Call for help."

Concern etched Bryce's features as his gaze

swung Richie's way. "Give it a second. It might not be anything to worry over."

Richie pushed away from the wall and paced. "I can't be trapped. Call for help." Even to his ears, Richie sounded anxious. A part of him recognized he could call, push buttons, or do any number of things to help himself. The rest of him was already in panic mode.

Thankfully, Bryce didn't make him ask a third time. He opened the call box and brought the phone to his ear. "Yeah, we're stuck."

"Don't say we're stuck," Richie said in a stage whisper. The fact that Bryce didn't roll his eyes said a lot about how good the man was at his job. Bryce was one of five shrinks who worked for the combined letters in the building—CIA, FBI, and DEA. That was one of the biggest reasons Richie had walked away from the man. He saw Richie too clearly. Richie knew he was overreacting. Fear was like that. It didn't give a shit what Richie knew. He'd been locked away in a room smaller than a closet for two months. There'd been enough room to sit, but not stretch out his legs. He couldn't stand or lie. It had been so dark he couldn't see his own hands, and Richie had been left with nothing but his thoughts. He couldn't be trapped again.

"They're working on it," Bryce said, cutting into his thoughts. "Are you okay?"

Richie stopped pacing long enough to focus his rage on Bryce. "Do not fucking psychoanalyze me right now, Bry. I'm not one of your patients."

A loud, tired-sounding sigh filled the elevator. It was unnecessary. Richie already knew he'd exhausted Bryce long ago. Why did he have to be trapped with Bryce of all people? He liked to think he'd win the man back someday. Days like today proved it would never happen. He couldn't stop being weak. Bryce was too smart to be tricked by Richie's false veneer of sanity. The man deserved to be with someone who could hold his shit together.

"Shit." Richie couldn't stop the curse from escaping. "I'm sorry."

"Don't apologize."

At Bryce's order, Richie focused on him. Bryce looked calm. Of course he was. It was his job to be cool and collected—to fix other people. "Don't say that," Richie argued. "I owe you several apologies. Fuck. What's taking so long?" Richie was two minutes shy of scratching off his skin. He already couldn't stop pacing.

"You should focus on something else," Bryce said, pushing away from the wall. Before Richie could guess at his intentions, Bryce overcame him. The cool wall touched his back as Bryce invaded his space. Richie couldn't look away, even as Bryce lowered his head. Their lips met. It happened without thought. Accepting Bryce's kiss was as natural as breathing. Everything else fell away. He no longer felt trapped. They were alone. The faulty elevator transformed into a haven. Bryce held Richie's bottom lip between his teeth, nibbling. Richie's hands found the man's waist. He missed everything about them. The backs of his eyes burned from the longing. Then Bryce opened his mouth over Richie's, and heat exploded through him. Their tongues brushed. The familiar taste of Bryce filled Richie's mouth. He wanted to pull away and beg Bryce to take him back, but the need to hold Bryce won. Bryce's hands slipped from clasping Richie's jaw to Richie's shoulders. He shuffled closer, deepening their kiss. Bryce's palms slid down Richie's arms before moving to his hips. Richie's heart sped. He knew Bryce's every move. His body tensed—expectant. His every fiber focused on the final inch between them, willing Bryce to make it disappear. He craved the sensation of Bryce's erection brushing his as they fought to get closer. Instead, Bryce moved away. A flush rode high on the man's cheeks, making his light eyes seem even lighter. Bryce swiped his thumb across Richie's bottom lip, wiping away the moisture from their kiss.

"This is your floor."

Richie's gaze shot to the open elevator door before shifting back Bryce's way. "I—"

"You should go before you're stuck again," Bryce said, cutting him off and sending him on his way.

With one final lingering look, Richie did as Bryce bade. He needed to think. They'd kissed. Richie wasn't sure he could go back to being without Bryce again. He might not have any choice. Richie had fucked things up between them pretty royally. Today was the first day in months that things didn't feel hopeless. Richie needed to ponder this and make a plan. He also needed to find an empty bathroom and jack off, but that was another story.

BRYCE'S HANDS SHOOK. He tried balling them into fists only to find his teeth chattered as well. Seeing Richie freaking out started Bryce on the road to losing his shit. Kissing the man had done him in. The five-floor ride to his office didn't help. It had been five months and three weeks since Richie walked away. In that time, Bryce had done his damnedest to move on and save himself. With one kiss, he'd wiped away all the progress Bryce had made. Goddamn, his cock ached. Every nerve ending in his body craved what only Richie could do for him. It had started on the train, with Richie standing only inches away. He'd felt Richie's stare like a physical touch. Now Bryce couldn't stop craving the real thing.

He had clients today—people who wanted to get better. Bryce would do well to focus his energy where it was wanted. As he took off his jacket, Bryce fought the urge to drop into his chair and put his head between his knees. The air felt too thin to sustain him. No one made him feel useless the way Richie did. The man didn't want Bryce—not his help or his love. Nothing had changed. Bryce would focus on work. His job was all he had.

Bryce made it through two clients and lunch at his desk before his mind found the topic of Richie once more. They'd met three years ago, in that same fucking elevator. Richie had been a field agent back then, and cocky as hell. Bryce's heart sped at the memory. He'd caught the man checking out his ass. Richie had smirked, daring Bryce with his eyes to call him out. Goddamn, their nights had been hot. Between Richie's confidence and dominance, he'd swept Bryce off his feet in no time. Bryce had fallen so damn hard and fast, all other men disappeared in his eyes. Then Richie had gone missing in the middle of an investigation. Chills raced over Bryce's skin. He couldn't even think about those days. Everything ended with Richie's disappearance. He'd come home a stranger Bryce still didn't recognize. Bryce's phone buzzed, pulling his thoughts from the dark place where he kept those memories buried. He dug out the device.

Richie: *We should have dinner.*

Bryce blinked at the face of his phone. It was the first text he'd gotten from Richie in ages. The final messages Bryce had sent Richie, begging the man to talk to him, were still hovering above the new text from Richie. The sight of his words, pleading for anything from Richie, kept Bryce from responding. All the pain burst through the thin wall he'd built around his heart. He swallowed past the lump in his throat. Bryce shut his phone inside his desk before his mind snapped. He'd never been more scared for the safety of an electronic device.

He wanted to chuck it against the wall. Bryce wasn't angry with Richie. Not really. He was mad at himself for being weak and craving Richie's touch. Bryce reached beneath his desk and readjusted his cock. It only ever took the thought of Richie to stir his blood. They had more memories together than Bryce could count. For some reason he couldn't explain, their night together before Richie had left for his final undercover op kept invading his mind. Bryce's hands had been handcuffed to the headboard. A dildo filled his ass. His dick filled Richie's mouth.

A light on his business line lit. "Dr. Macrae, Agent Christoph is here for his two o'clock."

"Please ask him to give me fifteen minutes," Bryce said, sounding as devastated as he felt. "I need to make a call."

"Yes, sir."

With his appointment on hold, Bryce headed for the private bathroom inside his office. Richie's face wouldn't leave his head. The memory of the man's hot mouth on Bryce's dick wouldn't abate. Bryce tried splashing his face with cold water. Nothing helped. The erection tenting his pants wouldn't go down. It wasn't fair for one person to own his body the way Richie did. The man knew all

Bryce's perversions and shared them. Bryce had been convinced they were soul mates. Everything about them had been perfect before it was ripped away.

Bryce stared at his reflection. He looked every bit as turned on as he was. Anyone who saw him would know. There was no denying the flush to his cheeks and the desperation in his eyes. His hand slid to his crotch once more. Bryce watched it happen in the mirror. His chest tightened as his palm made contact with his aching cock. He slid his zipper down and set his erection free. If there'd ever been a point of return, he'd missed it. Bryce needed release. His gaze never wavered from watching his crown disappear over and over again inside his fist. His eyes tried falling closed from the pleasure. He refused to shut out the sight. It was him pleasing himself. Richie wasn't there. He didn't need Richie's skilled mouth and wicked tongue. A ragged breath escaped Bryce. He didn't have to have Richie's palm stinging his ass to come. Bryce's muscles tensed. He no longer saw his palm on his dick. In his mind, Richie was in his knees. Bryce closed his eyes and let it happen. He pumped faster, reaching for the orgasm the fantasy of Richie's willing throat promised. His balls drew up tight.

Bryce braced his free hand against the bathroom sink to keep his knees from giving out. Tiny sparks of pleasure climbed up his shaft. Pressure beat at his crown. Ecstasy exploded through him. Bryce forced his eyes open as jets of semen hit the sink. He made himself see that it was him that brought himself to orgasm. Richie wasn't there. When the madness passed, Bryce was left feeling empty as he washed away his mess. He could no longer meet his own gaze in the mirror. This was what Richie had left behind. Bryce had needed the reminder.

He made his way back to his desk, doing his damnedest to feel nothing. He spent five minutes catching his breath before finally asking his receptionist to send in Agent Christoph. He smiled as the older and balding agent came through the door. Bryce made it through their hour together by making sympathetic faces in all the right places and offering suggestions. This was his day, helping others while he silently fell apart. He was certain, if anyone bothered looking close enough, they'd see he was a fraud.

Five more appointments and some paperwork later, Bryce burst from the building without looking back. He kept his gaze locked straight ahead, intentionally seeing no one. Never in Bryce's life had he been more afraid to meet anyone's gaze. He was one knowing look away from melting down. Bryce swore his lips still tingled from Richie's kiss. Maybe it was time for him to find something else. He could open a private practice. All his school loans had been paid off by the company in exchange for his services for five years. He'd been there eight. Bryce could move on. With a new job and some distance, maybe he could meet someone new. It had been hell knowing Richie was in the same building, five floors down. Bryce's pride had kept him from ever seeking the man out, but still. He'd known.

With an unofficial plan in place, Bryce's shoulders relaxed as he slid into the first empty seat he found on the train. He took a deep breath and then another. Sometimes breathing helped more than anyone realized. Bryce tried emptying his mind. Without thought, he brushed his bottom lip. Damn, he missed having someone to kiss him good night. Sometimes it was the little things that threatened his sanity.

"So, dinner tonight," Richie said, slipping into the empty space beside Bryce.

Bryce startled at the man's sudden appearance. He chewed the inside of his cheek to keep from growling. This was his fault. He never should've kissed Richie.

Richie didn't let up. "Come on. I'll buy."

"No, thanks." Before Richie could say more, and in a desperate attempt to escape, Bryce tapped a woman standing nearby. She was pregnant and didn't need to be stuck on her feet. When she turned his way, he flashed her a smile. "Take my seat."

"Thank you." She sounded relieved. Her grateful smile made giving up his spot worthwhile. Not to mention, he needed to get away from Richie. He exchanged places with the woman, moving away from Richie and holding on to the railing.

Richie followed. "Say yes, and I promise I won't text you every five minutes for the rest of the night."

"Was that a threat?" Even Bryce heard the laughter in his voice. Richie was the type to keep his word. If Bryce said no, Richie probably would text him every five minutes for the rest of the night.

Richie shrugged, looking way too sure of himself. "Whatever works. Have dinner with me."

Bryce turned his back on him without answering. A minute passed. His phone buzzed. Bryce dug it out.

Richie: *Please?*

The growl in his throat got harder to suppress. His phone buzzed again.

Richie: *Pretty please? I may even resist sending you a dick pic if you eat with me.*

Fuck his life. A smile pulled at his lips. This was the side of Richie that Bryce had fallen in love with. The man could be playful and persistent. Unfortunately, he could also be dark, brooding, and distant.

Bryce turned, ready to put Richie in his place. They were damn near nose to nose. The breath caught in Bryce's throat. Richie had the most gorgeous brown eyes. They were sweet and almost whisky in coloration. He'd stared into those eyes countless times under numerous circumstances— like when Richie had proposed, and when the man had broken him.

"Just dinner," he heard himself agree.

"And drinks?"

The growl won.

Richie smirked. "I could make you do that again under better circumstances."

Fuck him. Bryce knew it was true. "Just dinner," he repeated, determined to hold on to some control.

Richie's triumphant smile grew. "I'll drive."

"Whatever," Bryce said, uncaring. He just wanted this over with. They would have dinner, and then Bryce would go home. Alone. Then, tomorrow, he'd start looking into setting up his own practice. It was way past time he made a life for himself without Richie.

CHAPTER 2

CHOOSING BRYCE'S favorite steakhouse had been a purposeful move. No doubt, Bryce saw right through every play Richie made. Not that it mattered. Richie was in fight mode. From the instant Bryce's lips touched his in that elevator, Richie had been set on a new path. Bryce had given him purpose. Richie fully intended to win him. Nothing mattered since losing this man. He needed Bryce in his life and in his bed. Richie wouldn't stop until he had him.

"You're gorgeous."

Bryce kept his gaze locked on his menu like it contained the answers to life. "Thanks."

"Seriously," Richie said while trying not to laugh at Bryce's obvious discomfort. "Is that a new suit? I'm barely stopping myself from licking you."

Annoyance flashed in Bryce's eyes when he finally focused on Richie. "What are you doing?"

"Complimenting you," Richie said, sounding ridiculously chipper even to his ears.

"Please stop." Bryce went back to staring at the menu.

Richie's smile grew. He was having the time of his life. "No. Did you know, I stare at you every day. I didn't realize how much I was missing, back when I used to drive us to work. Just think, I could've spent those two years staring at you."

"Can I get you guys something to drink?"

"Thank fuck," Bryce muttered under his breath at the appearance of their waiter. "Could I get a sparkling water?"

"Beer," Richie said, placing his order without waiting to be asked. His gaze never wavered from Bryce.

Bryce shook his head. "You're driving. He'll have a sparkling water too."

"Got it," the waiter said, obviously uncaring of Richie's wishes. "Are you ready to order or do you need a few more minutes?"

"I'm ready," Bryce said, ensuring there could be no doubt he wanted this date over with.

Richie bit his lip, trying hard not to laugh. "I need a few more minutes."

Bryce rolled his eyes.

A soft chuckle escaped Richie.

The young waiter moved on, leaving them alone.

Richie let the silence grow, waiting. Finally, Bryce met his stare. A wave of longing overcame him. "Beau misses you."

A flash of hurt passed over Bryce's features. "I miss him too."

They'd adopted their husky mix, Beau, from a shelter not long after they moved in together. In truth, the dog preferred Bryce to anyone else in the world, but Bryce hadn't wanted Richie to be alone when he'd left. Sometimes, at the oddest moments, it would hit Richie—he'd truly stolen everything from Bryce. It was no wonder the man wanted this dinner to end.

"You should come by and see him sometime."

"Have you had time to decide?" the waiter asked, reappearing at the edge of the table.

"Yes," Bryce answered for them both before Richie could send him away again. "He'll have the sirloin with a loaded baked potato. I'll have the grilled chicken and rice. Thanks." He handed the man both the menus and sent him on his way.

Bryce's expression kept shifting from sad to angry. The man's eyes softened then hardened. Richie wished he could read minds. "You ordered chicken. At a steakhouse. Your favorite steakhouse," Richie added, because he couldn't stop.

"I stopped eating red meat last month after a kidney stone."

Richie winced. "Ouch. You should've called. I would've taken care of you."

Bryce's face went blank. He stared at Richie emotionlessly. Richie could practically hear the man mentally telling him to go fuck himself. As usual, Bryce stayed calm. "I took care of myself."

He couldn't explain why the words punched him in the chest, but they did. Maybe it was the realization of how deeply he'd failed Bryce. Richie would like to think he'd spoiled the hell out of Bryce when they'd been together. He'd let that tiny closet in Mexico beat him. Every day, when Richie woke up and didn't give Bryce the world, that space no bigger than a grave won. Richie may as well have died there.

Their food arrived and disappeared. Richie ate without tasting a bite. When he'd asked Bryce to dinner, there hadn't been time to plan. All he knew was he wanted the man back. Richie didn't have the first fucking clue how to do that. Their feet brushed under the table. Even though he was certain it had been an accident, Richie's gaze still shot to Bryce. Bryce watched him as if trying to figure out Richie's next move. Without any real plan in mind, Richie slid from the booth and shoved Bryce over. He intentionally took up more space than necessary, ensuring their thighs touched. Bryce didn't argue, but he also wouldn't look at Richie.

"Is there something wrong with your side of the table?"

Richie slung his arm across the back of the seat, moving even closer. "Yep. You're not over there. How about we stop by my place when we leave here so you can see Beau?"

"That seems unnecessarily cruel, since I'll probably never see him again." Bryce braced his hand against Richie's thigh when Richie tried shifting even closer. "Damn, how much space do you need?"

"I'll move back to the other side if you say you'll come see Beau."

Bryce didn't move his hand. His fingers stroked Richie's leg, making Richie wonder if Bryce even realized he'd done it. "I'll go see Beau if you let me pay."

Oh, that was sneaky. Bryce pulled out the big guns with that one. Richie hated it when Bryce paid for anything. The man had timed his attack like a pro. He was willing to let Richie have two things for one—he got to stay put and Bryce would go home with him. Bryce's smile said he knew exactly what he'd done. He stroked Richie's leg again. This time, his hand moved higher. Fuck it. He wanted Bryce to come home with him more than he cared to hang on to his pride.

"Deal."

Bryce's low, sexy laugh had Richie going hard. Richie fought the urge to slump in the seat, forcing Bryce's hand closer to his cock. "How bad did that sting?"

Richie took a slow breath through his nose, trying to temper his body's reaction. "You have no idea." Taking another chance, Richie moved his arm just enough he could brush his fingers down Bryce's arm. He couldn't tear his eyes away from Bryce. Even the way the man's hair caught the light fascinated Richie. "I—"

"I'll just leave this here," the waiter said, setting the check on the table and appearing at just the right moment, saving Richie from saying something stupid.

Bryce quickly snagged it as if he didn't trust Richie to keep his end of the bargain. He eyed the ticket and dug his wallet out. Richie never stopped trailing his fingers along Bryce's skin and Bryce didn't try stopping him. It felt like progress. After cramming some bills in the book the waiter left, Bryce shoved his wallet back inside his jacket pocket. "Are you ready?"

As much as Richie hated giving up his spot next to Bryce, he nodded and slid from the booth. He waited for Bryce and waved him ahead. Richie might have to give up his spot, sitting close to Bryce, but no way was he missing his chance to watch Bryce's ass as they walked to the car. Damn, it was perfect—round and firm. Bryce's ass had been the first thing Richie had noticed about the man when they'd met three years ago. He'd followed the man onto the elevator, hypnotized by the man's perfect globes. When Bryce had turned, catching him staring, Richie had brazened the moment out. He'd been in Bryce's bed that night, was living under the man's roof two months later, and they were engaged by Christmas. Richie hadn't wanted anyone else since the day they'd met. He was scared shitless that even if Bryce never took him back, Richie would never want anyone else again.

Thankfully, the drive to Richie's house wasn't a long one. Every second Richie wasn't touching Bryce felt like a step in the wrong direction. As he pulled into the driveway of his tiny two-bedroom rental, Richie wondered what Bryce thought of the place. It was nowhere near as big as the house they'd shared together. Not only did Richie not make anywhere near the money Bryce did, he hadn't been looking for anything permanent when he'd left Bryce. He'd intentionally found a house he could walk away from. Richie had never meant to live here as long as he had. In fact, he hadn't intended a lot of things.

"This is a quiet neighborhood," Bryce said, doing a damned good job of keeping his thoughts on the place hidden.

Richie nodded. "It is." He didn't know why he couldn't find something to talk about. It wasn't like he didn't have questions. Richie worried about Bryce's mother and wondered if Bryce ever found the jacket he lost. Fuck. He just wanted to hear about Bryce's day. Still, none of those questions left his lips.

At the first sight of Bryce, Beau lost his mind,

nearly knocking Bryce to the floor in his excitement. Bryce transformed before Richie's eyes. His bright smile kicked Richie in the chest. He wished Bryce was half as excited when he looked at Richie. Bryce hugged Beau and swiped his hands through the dog's fur while praising him. He sat on the couch and let the dog go nuts.

"I can't remember the last time you looked this happy about anything. Maybe that's why I left." Richie wanted to take the words back as soon as they left his lips, but he didn't. It wasn't fair. Bryce deserved better from him, but that was their problem. They'd stopped being real with each other a long time ago.

Shock crossed Bryce's features, turning to rage, before settling on unnatural calm. "I'm sorry you feel like I failed you. This was a bad idea."

"Oh, for fuck's sake," Richie snapped, incapable of standing another second where they weren't working toward fixing whatever was broken. He needed Bryce, but he also needed Bryce to stop feeling like he couldn't be himself anymore. "Speak your mind for once in your life."

"What's that supposed to mean?" Bryce said, keeping his tone bland.

"You're the company shrink, Bry. People have to

go through you when everything goes to shit, and you don't stop being that guy when you get home. Like right now, you want to rip me to pieces, but you won't," he said, never surer of anything. "I can name fifty. No. I can name a hundred times you should've torn me to shreds for being a piece of shit to you, but you won't. Yell at me, Bry. Tell me you hate me for coming home a fucked-up mess. Stop being the shrink who's scared you'll damage my fragile mind," he begged, because they'd never be whole unless Bryce stopped being a doctor for five minutes.

"I hate you," Bryce said, sounding calm, and giving Richie exactly what he'd asked for. It hurt more than he expected. "I hate you for not leaning on me," he added, catching Richie off guard. Unfortunately, Bryce didn't stop there. "When you came home, I would've taken you fucked up, missing limbs, and half alive if you would've really come home to me. You didn't, not really. I can understand you wanting me to rage. Then you can feel better about leaving me, but I won't. I won't let you make breaking me all about you. If you would've come home and let me love you, I would've loved you forever—zero psychoanalysis or judgment. But first you didn't come home in mind, and then you didn't come home at all, and you don't get to feel better about doing that shit to me. That's on you." Bryce stood, obviously through with pretending he could stomach Richie's presence. He rubbed Beau's head one last time before heading for the door. "Thanks for dinner," Bryce said without looking back. "I can find my way home."

Richie couldn't move. He watched Bryce walk away from him, and there was nothing he could do. Bryce's claims left him paralyzed. All the times he'd thought Bryce hated him for being weak, he'd never really believed Bryce hated him. Hearing those three words from Bryce's lips; it was devastating. Richie didn't know where to go from there.

BY THE TIME Bryce made it to the curb, the wind had gone from his sails. He'd told Richie he hated him. It had been his hurt and anger talking. He should turn around and take it back. Bryce couldn't. His anger might have fled, but his hurt was permanent. Tomorrow, he'd take a personal day and find a space to lease for his practice. Being too close to Richie and seeing him all the time was bad for Bryce's soul. He couldn't keep this up.

Bryce dug his phone out and pulled up the app to find a cab. As pissed off as he was, he couldn't walk to where he'd left his car at the Park and Ride. Fuck. He should've known better than to accept a date with Richie.

"Come on," Richie said, appearing behind him. "What kind of person would I be if I left you with no way back to your car?"

Bryce didn't look away from his phone. "The same type of person who left me to begin with."

Richie put his hand over Bryce's phone, leaving him no other choice but to look at him. He looked hurt. Goddamn it. Life wasn't fair. "Let me take you back to your car."

A growl that sounded aggravated, even to Bryce, rose in his throat. "Fine." He stomped to the passenger side of Richie's car and waited for him to unlock the door.

Richie reached past him and opened it. "I'm sorry."

"Shut up," Bryce said as he climbed in and stared straight ahead. Fuck him and his apologies. They came too late. As Richie drove, Bryce stared out the window. Horrible memories overcame him.

Their friends were there, carrying furniture from their house. Bryce stared at the sight in confusion. He didn't bother stopping them. If Bryce was being honest, he'd seen this coming. Richie didn't look at him the same way since coming home. No matter how hard Bryce tried to be the man Richie needed, Richie pulled further away.

Gathering his jacket, Bryce climbed from the car. No amount of stalling would make this easier. Wyatt and Darrel averted their eyes as he passed. He found Richie in the living room.

"I'd ask what's going on, but I'm not stupid."

Richie turned. His expression gave nothing away. "It's time."

Bryce focused on tossing his jacket on the couch to hide the way his eyes filled with tears. He cleared his throat. "Have you met someone else?"

Richie's voice was cold. "No."

Bryce nodded, still incapable of looking at him. "So you've just decided you don't love me anymore."

"No. I imagine I'll always love you."

Bryce blew out a sigh. He was so fucking tired. "Okay. You should take Beau. He's gotten used to you being home with him." Without another word or a backward glance, Bryce headed for the bedroom. Richie could leave. Bryce couldn't stop him. That didn't mean Bryce had to help him or watch it happen.

Richie was hot on his heels. "Beau is your dog."

"Not anymore," Bryce said without slowing.

Before he could close the door, Richie grabbed his hand, forcing Bryce to meet his gaze. Bryce wondered if this would kill him. Surely no one could hurt this much and live. The saddest part was, Richie was the one choosing to leave, and even he didn't look happy. "I've never left this house without kissing you goodbye."

Richie's claim was fire in Bryce's gut. He pulled his hand away. "Guess you'll have to start today," Bryce said as he closed the door in Richie's face. With the wooden surface between them, Bryce slid to the floor with his back against the door. The first tear fell. Bryce didn't bother wiping it away. He knew a million more would follow. Between Richie's disappearance and the man coming home a mess, Bryce hadn't thought of himself in ages. Now all he had was himself—what Richie left behind of him, that is.

"You broke my heart," Bryce said, incapable of staying silent a second longer as they pulled into the Park and Ride. "You broke my heart," he said a little stronger this time because it was worth repeating and needed to be said. "I don't know what tonight was all about, but if you came looking for more pieces of my heart to smash, you wasted your time. You crushed all of me a long time ago." He grabbed the door handle and met Richie's gaze. "Please stay away from me. I've got nothing left for you to take." Bryce leapt from the car before Richie could stop him. There was nothing left to say.

After climbing into his car, Bryce slammed the door with more force than necessary. He was furious. It wasn't that he hadn't been angry in the past. He had. This was something more—like the dam had finally burst inside him. He loved Richie. Probably he always would. Before tonight, he'd never considered the man cruel. Now Bryce wasn't so sure. There'd been no point to Richie's dinner offer. He'd obviously only wanted to hurt Bryce again—like taking everything hadn't been enough. When Richie's headlights disappeared, Bryce dropped his head to the steering wheel. Fuck all. He didn't know where to go with all his fury. Everyone expected him to be the strong one. Only one person had ever recognized he'd suffered too after Richie's disappearance. There was only one of their friends who didn't make Bryce feel guilty for needing help too.

Bryce dug out his phone.

Bryce: *Richie asked me to dinner. I went. It was bad.*

Thankfully, he got a response right away.

Jayden: *The food or the company?*

Bryce swiped at his cheeks and responded.

Bryce: *The company. The food was all right. Of course, I ended up paying, so I guess that part sucked too.*

Jayden: *LOL! Sucker. Need some company?*

Bryce: *Yes! Thank you. I'm still fifteen minutes from home. Meet me there?*

Jayden: *Sounds good. Don't text and drive.*

Bryce: *I'm not. We took Richie's car from the Park and Ride. I'm sitting in my car here.*

Jayden: *Okay. Be careful. Love you.*

Bryce: *Love you too. See you in a few.*

With a plan in place that didn't include Bryce being alone, Bryce finally started his car. He swiped at his face again, wiping away more tears he didn't realize had fallen. One of these days, he'd stop letting Richie fuck him up. He'd grow some balls or build a wall, something that would help him let the man go. Some days, it seemed impossible. Every night, he still thought about Richie as he climbed into the bed they'd shared. Every morning, he reached for the man, only to find his spot empty. Six months, and it never got easier. His house came into view, making Bryce realize Jayden had been right to worry over his safety. He didn't recall a second of the drive.

Bryce parked in the garage and didn't move. He already knew what he'd find inside—five bedrooms and four bathrooms. All of them empty of life. When he'd been a child, he'd lived three streets over in a house twice this size. No happiness had lived in that house either. His parents had gotten divorced back when Bryce was too little to remember. That separation didn't stop their fights. They fought over money, visitation, and his father's mistresses. His mother's younger lover. He loved them for the opportunities they'd given him in life, but he wasn't entirely sure they'd ever really loved him. They loved fighting. He'd given them purpose. Now, they barely spoke. Bryce had met and dated several men before Richie, but Richie was the first person who made him feel loved. He'd tried burying himself in work since Richie left, but all he felt was empty.

After climbing from the car, Bryce made his way inside. He barely turned on the light inside the kitchen before he found a bottle of wine. Jayden probably wouldn't drink. He rarely did. Even though—like Bryce—the guy had plenty of reason. Unlike Jayden, Bryce had parents, such as they were. Jayden had no one. Like Bryce, Jayden loved someone who didn't love him back. It was a hell of a place to be. A knock landed on the front door as Bryce turned up the bottle, forgoing the glass. He took another swig as he moved to let Jayden in.

Jayden wore baggy jeans, a white t-shirt, and an open flannel. Too bad. Jayden was an EMT and Bryce kind of liked staring at a man in uniform. They were only friends, but hot was hot and sexiness made Bryce happy. He waved Jayden inside while turning the bottle up again.

"You want some?"

"Only if I can stay the night."

Bryce passed the bottle Jayden's way. "Of course. Drink up. God knows I have plenty."

Jayden downed some of the bottle while closing the door behind him. "Damn. This date must've been bad."

"It wasn't a date," Bryce said, heading back to the kitchen. He grabbed another bottle, allowing Jayden to keep the other. "I'm not sure what it was. We had dinner and went back to his place, so I could see Beau," Bryce clarified before Jayden jumped to any conclusions. "The conversation went downhill right away, and I told him I hate him." Bryce eyed the wine glasses hanging from the rack. Fuck it. He turned up the bottle.

"How did you end up on a date to begin with?" Jayden set his empty bottle on the counter.

Bryce blinked at it, and then handed Jayden another. It looked like they'd be getting fucked up tonight. "We got stuck in the elevator together this morning, and he sort of flipped out over being trapped. I kissed him. Don't ask why. It just seemed the thing to do at the time. Anyhow." Bryce polished off his bottle before speaking again. "He asked me to dinner and I had a moment of weakness." He eyed the two empty bottles on the counter. "We need something stronger. You up for something stronger?"

Jayden shrugged while still sipping on his second bottle. "You already said I could stay. I say, let's do it right. Plus, I don't have to be at work until one tomorrow."

"I'm taking a personal day tomorrow," Bryce said absently as he dug through the freezer for the two bottles of Jack he had inside. They'd never been opened. "Which reminds me, since you're staying, do you want to go with me to look at office spaces in the morning?"

Jayden set his wine aside. His gorgeous green gaze moved over Bryce's face. "Damn. Things did go bad. Are you really going through with quitting your job?"

Bryce passed one of the whiskey bottles Jayden's way, grabbed two glasses, and headed for the living room. "Yeah. I can't do this anymore. Knowing he's in the same building, it's stopping me from starting over." Bryce plopped down on the couch. The soft leather cradled him in his time of need. "Fuck. I hate everything. How are you?" Bryce asked, feeling like shit for dumping on Jayden the instant the man walked through the door.

Jayden shrugged and took up the spot next to Bryce, sitting so close their thighs touched. They had so much in common. The two of them needed affection. They wilted without it, so they got it from each other. Jayden took the glasses and poured them each a hefty drink. "I ran into Wyatt yesterday. He tells me Darrel had surgery on his shoulder. That's how I find out everything these days—secondhand." Jayden was ten years younger than Bryce. He was fourteen years younger than Darrel. That hadn't stopped Jayden from falling in love with the jackass. Darrel was one of those guys —too much confidence, too sexy for his own good, and never wanted what he could have. The man had pined for and chased after Jayden until he landed him. The moment he'd known he owned Jayden, he'd broken Jayden's heart. Unfortunately, that seemed to be Jayden's calling in life. He was young and sexy. Men wanted him, but they never wanted to keep him. They liked to have him and then move on, leaving him brokenhearted. Bryce liked him better than most people. It helped they were a lot alike. Bryce cared too much about people's mental health to the point he neglected his own. Jayden cared about people's physical health, even when that person didn't care if he lived or died.

"I wish there was something I could say," Bryce said, taking a huge gulp of his whiskey. It burned. He relished the pain.

Jayden chugged his drink like he was at a frat party, proving his mood was every bit as shitty as Bryce's. He sucked in a gasp when the glass was empty. "Me too. You know what, I miss kissing. Like, I know that sounds stupid, but I can't help it. I miss days of lounging in bed, doing nothing except stealing kisses and being lazy. You'd think I expect the moon, considering how perpetually single I always am."

"That's not stupid at all," Bryce argued. "I had a similar thought earlier. Yeah, Richie was freaking out and everything, but I'm sure I could've talked him around. Kissing him was selfish. I miss affection, I guess."

"I'll kiss you," Jayden said, pulling a chuckle from Bryce. Jayden waved a dismissive hand. "No,

I'm serious. Let's go to bed. I'll kiss you, and we can be lazy. We don't need anyone else."

Bryce flashed Jayden a grateful smile. "You're amazing. But I don't love you like that."

Jayden shrugged. "No one does, so what's the harm?"

Outrage hit Bryce in the chest. He wasn't mad at Jayden. Bryce was pissed at the universe on the man's behalf. He was amazing. "You deserve someone who loves you. I've known you for a long time, and you've never gotten even half the awesomeness you should. Fuck Darrel. I hope his arm falls off."

A slow smile spread across Jayden's face before a bark of laughter escaped him. "You don't hope that."

"Maybe I do," Bryce said with an offended-sounding snort. He was tired of being perfect all the time. He always did his best, gave his all, and wanted the most for everyone else. Nice guys finished last. He was tired of being one of the good guys. Probably it was liquid courage driving him, but Bryce was ready to break some shit. He dipped his chin in a sharp nod, coming to a decision. "Okay, you can kiss me."

Jayden laughed, obviously thinking Bryce was

joking. "You're too good for me." As the final word left Jayden's lips, the happiness bled from the man's eyes. Bryce realized he meant it. Jayden honest to god believed he wasn't good enough to be loved.

Bryce needed Jayden to know that wasn't true. "If there was anything left of my heart, I'd love you. I'm smart enough to recognize a good thing." Bryce swallowed past the lump growing in his throat. "It's just that, first Richie went missing, and I'd thought I'd die. Then, he came home and he wasn't him any longer. The past year has broken me in ways I didn't know were possible. But, if I could, I would love you so hard you'd never want anyone else. You're worth it."

Jayden blinked and looked away. He visibly swallowed. "It should've been us. We should've met a long time ago."

"Agreed," Bryce said, holding out his arm. "Now come here."

Jayden dutifully settled against Bryce's side, allowing Bryce to cuddle him. Jayden turned his chin up. Bryce touched his lips to Jayden's. It wasn't unusual for them to kiss. Quick pecks between friends. That was all they'd ever be. This time, Bryce didn't pull away. Neither did Jayden. Bryce had meant what he said. If things were different, he'd give Jayden a real shot. He honestly didn't believe they'd ever hurt each other. They might not ever be a grand love affair, but they'd be comfortable and they did love each other. Jayden's mouth opened over Bryce's bottom lip. Bryce opened for him. Their tongues met, and Bryce let everything go. For once, it was nice to be kissed, even if it meant nothing. Maybe especially since it meant nothing. There were no hard feelings or scars between them. Jayden was his best friend, and no matter what else, the man would still be his friend tomorrow. Tonight, Bryce accepted Jayden's harmless affection. Maybe he wasn't Richie, but maybe that was a good thing.

CHAPTER 3

BRYCE WASN'T on the train. After some veiled questioning of his co-workers, Richie learned Bryce hadn't come in to work. Richie wanted to leave right that second and hunt the man down, but to what avail? Bryce had asked him to stay away. Even though Richie knew he wouldn't do that, he still didn't think showing up on the man's front steps and demanding to know why he hadn't come to work was a good way to fix things. He needed help. Richie needed a friend.

He called the only person he knew he could count on. Luckily, Darrel answered on the second ring. "Hey, how's it going?"

Proving he was a good friend, Darrel didn't exclaim his surprise over hearing from Richie for the first time in forever. "Hey. I can't complain. How are things going with you?"

There was no answering that question without lying, so Richie dodged it. "Do you have plans for lunch?"

"Nope."

"You want to meet at the diner?"

"Sure," Darrel said. Thankfully, he didn't sound the least bit put out. If he had, Richie might've changed his mind. Being around his friends was hard. He didn't like looking weak. Richie wasn't sure he'd been anything but since he returned to real life. "It'll take me about fifteen minutes to get there."

Richie nodded, forgetting for a minute Darrel couldn't see him. "Cool. It'll probably take me about the same. See you there."

"See you," Darrel said, disconnecting their call.

Richie stood and hoped he didn't back out. His friends had all tried being there for him. Richie had shut everyone out. Today, he really needed some advice.

On the walk to the diner, an unwelcome thought hit Richie. He hoped Darrel didn't call the whole gang together for lunch. Once upon a time, Darrel,

Wyatt, Jayden, and Richie had been inseparable. They each worked in high-pressure jobs as different public servants. Darrel and Wyatt were SWAT. Jayden was an EMT and Richie did what he did. They ran in the same circles and used to spend a ton of time together. Then Richie had come home from Mexico fucked up. Shortly after, Wyatt had gotten shot several times in the line of duty. The man met his husband that day. Then, Jayden and Darrel had started dating and everything between the four sort of shifted. Or, maybe it hadn't. Hell, Richie didn't know. They still did shit together—lunches, parties at Wyatt's mom's, since she might as well be all their mom. The four of them, now five with Wyatt's husband Benny, they were still friends. Maybe Richie just felt like the odd man out now. Whatever it was between them, Richie didn't feel like part of the group anymore. He didn't want to see them today. Darrel was the one he'd always felt closest to. If Richie planned to get back to normal, he needed to start there.

Thankfully, as he came through the door, he spotted Darrel sitting alone in a booth. He slid in across from him.

"Damn, man. What's with the get-up?" Richie

asked, motioning toward the sling Darrel wore on his left arm.

Darrel glanced down like he'd forgotten he had an injured wing. "I tore out a rotator cuff at the gym."

"How long are you stuck in that thing?"

"About six weeks. I'm also trapped with desk duty." Darrel didn't sound happy about it.

"That's a feeling I know all too well," Richie grumbled. He imagined his days of being in the field were over. No one had said as much, but they didn't need to.

Darrel nodded and picked up a menu. He spoke while focused on it. "I imagine. You should think of joining SWAT. We rarely see any action." He cleared his throat, moving on, and not giving Richie time to point out that Wyatt had almost died recently. "I have to say, I was a little surprised to hear from you. You haven't exactly come around much lately."

While focused on his menu, it wasn't as awkward to talk about shit. "I haven't felt like myself for a while. Sometimes, it's easier to be alone. But I'm still around. You're still my friend. I should've known about the shoulder."

Darrel snorted. "It's just a shoulder. Nothing I

can't handle alone. You've earned the right to deal with your shit your way. I'm just glad to see you out."

Richie nodded and chewed cn his lip. Honest to god, he didn't know where to start. "I saw Bryce last night." His lips moved without his brain's permission, jumping in with both feet.

"I would think you see him every day, working in the same building and all."

"We went to dinner."

Darrel dropped his menu and focused on Richie. "How did that go?"

"Well, he didn't spit in my face, but he did verbally destroy me and storm out."

To Richie's surprise, Darrel chuckled. "Good for him. It's about time he stood up for himself."

"I thought that at first too," Richie said, going back to staring at the menu. "I wanted him to get mad and stop being a psychologist for five seconds. Turns out, I wasn't prepared for what he had to say."

Darrel took the menu from Richie's hands, setting it aside and leaving him no other choice but to meet his stare. "Why would you want Bryce to stop being the psychologist? Bryce can't stop helping people. That's not a bad thing."

"It is when you're in my shoes."

Darrel leaned forward in his seat. His gaze fixed upon Richie, making Richie feel like the man had all the answers in the universe. "You're not hearing me. Bryce helps people. It's not what he does. That's who he is. If you want him back, you have to get on the same page. I know you want him to see you as a whole man, but be honest with yourself—are you? Whole, I mean?"

"No." It was funny how he admitted the truth so easily to Darrel when his voice wouldn't work with Bryce.

"Then you have to be real with him," Darrel said, leaning back in his seat and draping his arm across the back of the bench. "You're not less of a man for what you went through. I guarantee Bryce doesn't think you're weak. Not to mention, I'm sure you have other ways you can show him you're still in charge," Darrel said with a smirk. "Let the guy have all of you or stay away. I love you, man, but it's not right to hurt him again. Boy loves you for real, and leaving him the way you did was some cold shit." Darrel held up his free hand, as if he expected Richie would take offense. "I'm not saying I don't feel you. You thought you were saving him from you. But don't go back if you plan to rip his heart out again just because he can't stop being who he is, and you're no longer who you once were."

Richie heard him. He said everything a true friend should. Richie hadn't been in the right when he left. That didn't mean it didn't sting a little to hear it from Darrel. "What about Jayden and you?" Richie asked, needing his pound of flesh. "Everyone's dying to know why he doesn't come around anymore, but you don't talk about it." Jayden had been the one for Darrel. Everyone knew it. Richie sat back in surprise as Jayden appeared out of nowhere, as if talking about the man conjured him.

"Hey," Jayden said without an ounce of hesitation over whether his presence was welcome, even though Darrel looked like he might bolt. The guy shoved his way into the booth next to Darrel. Richie bit his lip to keep from laughing. Jayden was young and hot. Both Richie and Darrel were thirty-eight—much too old for Jayden's twenty-four-year-old ass. That hadn't stopped Darrel from falling for the guy. Not that Richie didn't understand. Jayden was sexy. He was skinny and tall with gorgeous green eyes. His soft-looking brown hair had the perfect amount of curl. While wearing his EMT uniform, everyone stared at Jayden, especially since

—like Darrel—the man possessed an overabundance of self-confidence. Both men knew they could have anyone they wanted. It was like the universe recognized it as fact, and no one could stop staring, looking for their opening. It seemed fitting they should love each other. Crazy they couldn't get on the same page.

Jayden inspected Darrel's hand that hung from the sling. He squeezed the tips of Darrel's fingers. "How's your circulation been?"

Darrel accepted Jayden's inspection without argument. The man's gaze moved over Jayden's face. Desperation coated the air. "Fine. I've been doing everything the surgeon suggested."

Jayden nodded while keeping his gaze carefully averted, as if scared to meet Darrel's stare. "That's good. Just text me if anything starts feeling strange."

"I should've told you."

Jayden stood, calling an end to whatever Darrel had been about to say. His gaze slid Richie's way. Richie swallowed. There was so much in the man's eyes. Richie couldn't process it all. "Richie. It's been a while."

"It's good to see you."

Jayden's expression turned cold and mocking. "I

can't say the same." Without a backward glance, Jayden walked away.

Richie watched him go. The man slid into a booth where another EMT sat. Richie met Darrel's stare. The man's mouth was lifted in one corner. "What the fuck was that?"

"Bryce got custody of him in the split," Darrel answered. Laughter swam in his eyes. "Jayden is loyal to the bone. If I were you, unless you win back Bryce soon, I wouldn't need an ambulance anytime in the near future. It might not arrive in time."

"Jesus," Richie breathed. Things just kept getting better and better.

Darrel wouldn't stop staring at Jayden like the world was crashing down.

Richie couldn't take it. "Follow your own advice," Richie urged. "Go talk to him. Make things right."

"I can't fix what I did," Darrel said, sounding absent. "Besides, he has a hickey. Seems I've lost my chance."

Richie glanced over his shoulder. Sure enough, there was a small but obvious hickey on Jayden's neck. Richie shrugged. "That doesn't mean much. It definitely doesn't mean you've lost your shot."

Without tearing his gaze away from Jayden,

Darrel shook his head. His pain was almost tangible. "Some shit you can't take back." He finally focused on Richie, looking more intense than Richie had ever seen him. "Go fix things with Bryce before you pull some shit you can't take back. Not all of us have that luxury."

Richie would do his damnedest. He couldn't end up feeling how Darrel looked—hopeless.

RICHIE: *I'm sorry.*

Bryce: *Apology accepted.*

Richie: *Can we talk?*

Bryce: *I'm sure I asked you to leave me alone.*

Richie: *I know.*

Richie: *I saw Jayden earlier.*

Bryce: *Okay.*

Richie: *He hates me now.*

Bryce: *Hate is a strong word. But you got everyone else. You have no right to complain.*

Richie: *I didn't mean to steal anyone from you.*

Bryce: *If someone can be stolen, they were never worth having. Plus, you need them more than I do. I'm used to being alone.*

Richie: *Fuck. I hate it when you say things like that. You deserve better from everyone, including me.*

Bryce: *Life doesn't give a fuck about "deserve." You get what you get. Besides, I have Jayden. Despite what everyone thinks of him, because of the whole Wyatt and Darrel thing, he's worth more than ten friends. Especially a cheat like Darrel.*

Richie: *Wow. It sounds like the two of you are closer than I realized.*

Bryce: *What of it? No one else has been around.*

Richie: *I'd like to be.*

Bryce: *Fuck off. I don't need someone who leaves me with no explanation, and is constantly angry with me for being myself. If you can't love me for me any longer, what's the point?*

CHAPTER 4

RICHIE NEVER TEXTED BRYCE BACK, and really, that answered Bryce's question. There was no point. No doubt, Richie was horny. Bryce was convenient. Well, fuck him. Bryce didn't intend to be convenient for anyone. He'd almost chosen to drive today, hoping to avoid seeing Richie again. The extra money, time, and hassle it took to drive each day almost outweighed the bullshit of being on the train with Richie. In the end, Bryce chose to ignore him. He knew he could do it. After all, he'd been pretending he didn't feel Richie's stare for the past six months. Today would be no different. Plus, it was only temporary. Soon, he'd have his own office set up, and he'd never see Richie again. Without thought, Bryce rubbed his chest. Emptiness gnawed at him.

Bryce stared at his folded newspaper, seeing nothing. Most people read their news on their phones. Bryce still preferred a real paper. Plus, it gave him something to focus on other than the sensation of Richie's stare stroking his skin. An unexpected smile touched his lips. It had always been the same back when they lived together. Bryce would feel Richie watching him from across the kitchen table in the mornings. Sometimes, he deliberately stoked the man's interest, teasing him. Their morning coffee separated them. Time slipped away...

"Goddamn, you're sexy."

Bryce forcibly rearranged his features, hiding his smile before dropping the paper and meeting Richie's gaze. "What?"

Richie leaned back in his chair and crossed his arms. His heated gaze slid down Bryce's body. "You know what you're doing, sitting there shirtless and chewing your bottom lip. I think you're asking for it."

Bryce's dick stirred. His thin pajama pants offered him no protection. All Richie needed to do was look, and he'd see how badly Bryce wanted him. "Asking for what? I'm just doing the crossword and minding my business."

"Uh-huh," Richie hummed. His disbelief coated the air. Bryce fought his smile. "What?"

Richie shifted to his feet. "If you're not after anything, then you won't care if I take Beau for a walk."

"Why would I care?" Bryce asked, keeping his gaze averted and his tone bland. "I'll just be here. Alone. Doing whatever." He emphasized each word, infusing as much heat as possible in his tone, leaving no doubt his hand would be on his hard dick if left alone.

"Tease," Richie growled. That was all the warning Bryce got before he was face down, bent over the table with Richie's cock filling his ass. They'd always been explosive together. Bryce rarely knew how he ended up getting fucked. All he knew was Richie filled his life with so much happiness, Bryce could barely breathe from the emotions choking him. Sometimes, he feared it was all a dream.

It had been, and waking from the illusion Richie painted him had been a nightmare that still wouldn't end.

"Amends."

Bryce's heart slammed against the wall of his chest as Richie appeared from nowhere and spoke against his ear. Without thought, he turned his head. Their gazes met. The light hit the man's sexy brown eyes at just the right angle, showing off their many facets. A smile touched Bryce's lips without his permission. "What?"

Richie winked. Bryce's heart fluttered, skipping

a beat at the sight. "A six-letter word for fixing things—amends." Bryce didn't ask how Richie had known he was looking at the crosswords. Not that Richie gave him time. "As in, I'm really sorry I ruined dinner the other night. Would you let me make it up to you tonight?"

"No, thank you," Bryce said, going back to staring at his puzzle.

"I could cook this time."

Fuck. He loved Richie's cooking.

"Tilapia," Richie said, sweetening the deal.

Goddamn it. That was his favorite.

Richie didn't let up. "You could spend some quality time with Beau while I take care of everything."

Shit. The man knew his stuff. Bryce had missed Beau twice as hard since seeing him the other night. Bryce cleared his throat. He didn't know how to give in gracefully. "Do you need me to bring anything?" He didn't look Richie's way. Bryce couldn't see the man's triumph. All Bryce felt was defeated. It seemed he would never stop letting Richie wreck him. It was like he was stuck in a time loop, repeatedly reliving the days when Richie broke his heart.

"Just show up." Richie's sad tone had Bryce

turning his head. There wasn't a hint of elation in Richie's expression. "I just need you to show up," Richie repeated, making Bryce wonder if the words had a double meaning. The psychologist in him couldn't stop reading into everything. If Richie needed Bryce to keep beating himself against the rocks to save him, he'd come to the right place. If he'd asked sooner, Bryce would've dogged the man's heels every day, invading the man's space, until Richie was whole.

"Tell me a time. I'll be there."

Richie's gaze moved over his face, searching. "Eight."

"I'll be there," Bryce repeated, hoping Richie caught his double meaning as well. As long as Richie needed him, Bryce would come, and that said all Bryce needed to know about how fucked up he was. He loved Richie and always would. If he didn't run soon, he'd let this man destroy him— over and over again until the end of time. If Richie needed and loved him for who he was, Bryce would never quit him.

THE TWO HOURS between work and Bryce's arrival for dinner were hell. Richie knew what needed to be done. He hoped he didn't lack the courage. He'd spent the whole night awake after having lunch with Darrel, thinking about the man's advice. His friend was right. Bryce's brilliant mind and caring heart were a huge part of why Richie loved him. If Bryce had stopped trying to save Richie, it wouldn't have stopped Richie from leaving. In fact, he might have left sooner. Together or not, Bryce saved him. Every day Bryce woke up, existing somewhere in the world, he gave Richie a reason to keep going. As long as Bryce was out there, there was hope.

When Bryce finally knocked on the door, Richie had to stop himself from running to answer. If he couldn't control his excitement over knowing Bryce was there, he had no clue how he ever thought he could live without the man forever. Bryce still wore his work clothes. The dark suit made Bryce's light eyes seem lighter. His green tie made them pop. Fuck. He was so goddamn beautiful.

"Sorry," Bryce said, sounding apologetic as he took off his jacket. "I had some business after work and didn't have time to change."

"It's fine." Richie stole his chance to kiss Bryce's

cheek before he could get away. "I'll take you any way I can get you. Plus, you're sexy as hell in your work clothes," he said, heading for the kitchen. "And out of them," he added under his breath. A low chuckle followed him, letting Richie know Bryce heard. Beau wasn't going insane, as he had the other night, but he was walking at Bryce's side, attached to his leg.

Bryce sat down at the kitchen table when Richie moved to the stove. Even with his back to Bryce, Richie knew every move Bryce made. Beau shoved his head in Bryce's lap, begging for all Bryce's attention. While Bryce loved on him, Beau whined nonstop in husky-speak. No doubt, he complained about everything Richie did—like not letting him sleep on the bed or drink from the toilet. Bryce made noises in all the right places, sympathizing with the dog's complaints.

"I told you he misses you," Richie said over his shoulder. "He's not the only one," he added as he fixed their plates.

Bryce moved to the sink and washed his hands. "This hasn't been easy for anyone."

Richie set their plates aside and crowded Bryce against the counter. He didn't let his hips touch Bryce's ass. That wouldn't be fair, but he did brush his lips across the man's nape before quickly backing away. Tonight wasn't about seduction. Not really. They needed to talk. Bryce made it damn hard for Richie to keep his hands to himself.

"Do you need my help with anything?" Bryce's voice sounded strained, but he kept his gaze locked on drying his hands.

Richie nodded toward the table. "Just go sit down. I've got this."

Bryce sat.

Beau settled between the man's feet.

Richie set a plate in front of him before claiming the chair across from him. "I hope everything is okay. To be honest, I don't cook that often any longer."

"It smells amazing. Thank you." Bryce took a bite. "Oh my god," Bryce said around his bite, looking orgasmic. "So good."

Richie watched him eat. Everything Bryce did was sexy. The way his jaw moved fascinated Richie. He loved every nuance of Bryce. He waited, not touching his food until Bryce was almost finished to strike. It took him that long to work up his nerve.

"I left you because I planned to kill myself and I didn't want you to have to deal with it."

Bryce froze.

Richie didn't stop, because there was no going back now. "I love you. Never stopped, but I convinced myself you were better off without me. I didn't come home the same. Every day I tried to be normal for you, and each day I failed until I knew I should stop waking up and let you be free of me."

The degree was gone. Bryce visibly struggled to rearrange his features, hiding his shock and hurt. He cleared his throat. "Um. What changed your mind?"

Richie's eyes fell closed for a moment. As much as he'd tried to prepare for this conversation, remembering those first days hurt. "I had to wait. If I died right away, you'd still be hurt. Then, I started back to work and spotted you on the train. You looked every bit as wrecked as I felt, so I watched and waited. I thought, I'll wait until I see him smile and mean it, then I'm done. So, every day I stared at you, watching. Then, one day I realized I wasn't looking at you any longer, hoping you'd smile. I was staring at you, hoping you'd look my way. Dr. Lowe said you gave me hope for the future. When he said that, I realized, it's always been you. When I was in hell, you were there. I thought of you every second and fought to stay alive so I could get back to you. Nothing has changed. Leaving didn't steal your power over me. You're still the reason I fight. It's not easy, Bry." Richie's throat swelled, cutting off his words. He swallowed and tried again because Bryce still hung on every word. "This loss of normalcy and mental peace, it's fucking destroyed me, but losing you has decimated what little I had left when I came home. But I had to leave you to find my way back."

Bryce stood and carried his plate to the sink. Beau followed. Once there, Bryce didn't move. He stared out the tiny window above the sink. Richie knew it was too dark for the man to see a thing other than what was inside his head. His insides shook, waiting for Bryce to speak. Bryce pushed away from the sink and wrapped his arms around Richie's shoulders from behind. With his face buried against Richie's neck, Bryce spoke as if fighting back tears. "I know you don't feel it and there's nothing I can say to change your mind, but you haven't told me anything you couldn't have said to me at any time. For what's it worth, I love you. I didn't mean what I said the other night." After pressing a kiss to Richie's neck, Bryce headed for the door, as if he meant to leave. Richie shot to his feet.

With no real plan in mind, Richie sprang. He

snagged Bryce's arm before the man could get away. With a tug, he had Bryce in his arms. His mouth hit Bryce's with enough force their teeth bumped. Heat mixed with Richie's fear, creating a volatile mix. He loved Bryce and missed him. Richie knew it was all his fault. He knew he'd shut Bryce out and slowly choked the life from his love. Richie couldn't pretend he wasn't to blame for everything. He'd thrown away a good man. Bryce kissed him back every bit as desperately. They were perfect together.

"I miss you," Richie said before going deep and doing his damnedest to lick the roof of Bryce's mouth. "I'm so fucking sorry. For everything. Goddamn. I miss everything about you," he admitted as he grabbed two handfuls of Bryce's ass and hauled the man against him. Bryce was hard for him. Their erections bumped. Bryce pulled Richie's shirt up and over his head before kissing Richie back every bit as fiercely. No one understood how much he'd missed Bryce's kisses. Of all the hundreds of reasons Richie thought he might be truly insane, this was the biggest one—losing Bryce. Losing him had been the hardest experience of Richie's life. It wasn't the drug kings or the months he spent trapped. Being without Bryce topped all other pain.

Bryce unbuttoned his shirt and tried pulling his tie over his head. Richie tried to help, but he couldn't give up Bryce's mouth for long. "I really fucking need you." Richie had always had a problem keeping his mouth shut when he was turned on. "I want you straddling my face and my dick."

Bryce unbuckled his belt while kissing Richie's jaw. "Pick one. I can't do both at the same time."

"Face first," Richie said, helping Bryce out of his clothes before taking him to the floor. Beau tried shoving his way between them, obviously thinking it was time to play. "Okay, this won't work. Come on," he said, rolling back to his feet and grabbing Bryce's hand. He headed for the bedroom. Richie locked Beau out, and then he took the opportunity to strip off the rest of his clothes. "On the bed."

Bryce did as ordered. His flushed face and swollen lips held Richie prisoner. He needed to keep Bryce right where he was, willing to do anything for the pleasure Richie offered. Damn, his man was beautiful and Richie would never stop thinking of Bryce as his. Bryce had a runner's body—tight and perfect. Richie needed to lick it.

"Damn, you're so fucking amazing."

He crawled onto the bed and dragged his tongue from Bryce's hip to his nipple. Richie paused to nip at the pink bud. He heard the breath catch at the back of Bryce's throat. An evil smile tugged at Richie's lips. His cock ached. Richie palmed his erection, stroking once and hoping to ease some of the building pressure. Nothing mattered as much as pleasing this man who watched him with lust in his eyes. Richie knew every inch of Bryce's body and exactly how to make him scream. He hovered above Bryce, dragging out the anticipation before brushing his lips against Bryce's in the lightest kiss. He couldn't give Bryce satisfaction. Not yet. The man's lust was the only thing keeping him there. Richie didn't fool himself by thinking otherwise. Bryce was still upset with Richie for shutting him out. Richie would fix everything. He kissed the man's chin and then his Adam's apple, making his way down Bryce's body. He couldn't undo the past. Richie wasn't healed. Bryce didn't deserve his bullshit. None of that changed a damn thing. Richie loved Bryce. He hated being without him. If Bryce would take him—broken or not, as he claimed, Richie wanted him to. Richie shifted lower, tonguing the spot beneath Bryce's breastbone. Bryce's fingers found Richie's hair. He held on.

"That's it, sexy. Take what you want," Richie urged, moving lower.

Bryce's ragged breaths sounded loud in the otherwise silent room. "Stop teasing," Bryce begged.

Richie didn't let up. "Demand what you need."

Bryce's hold tightened on Richie's hair. "I can already feel your hot mouth on my dick. Let me have it."

A roar of satisfaction rang through Richie's mind as he gave in and opened his mouth over Bryce's cock. This wasn't about control or having his way. He'd needed Bryce's verbal admission of wanting him. Richie teased the sensitive nerve endings in Bryce's crown before taking the man down his throat. He hollowed out his cheeks and sucked, reveling in the sounds Bryce made. Bryce's hips left the bed. Richie let the man fuck his willing mouth. Pre-cum coated his tongue. A moan escaped Richie at Bryce's flavor—salt and man. Damn, he was delicious. Richie's dick leaked. Desire ruled him. He didn't care about anything except making Bryce come so he could get inside him. Richie moved lower, fisting Bryce's cock while licking the man's balls. He urged Bryce's thighs farther apart, making room for him to tongue the man's asshole. Bryce writhed beneath him, making sounds that drove Richie insane.

"I want you inside me."

Bryce's confession snapped Richie's control. He flew to his knees and dove for the bedside table, coming out with a condom and lube. In a matter of seconds, he was suited up and had two oiled fingers inside Bryce's ass. Richie stared down at Bryce. The man's unfocused gaze and parted lips painted the sexiest picture Richie had ever seen. His stomach muscles clenched with his need to take Bryce—hard.

"Please?"

Richie broke at Bryce's plea. He captured the man's lips as he shoved his way inside. Once fully seated, Richie froze. Bryce was too perfect—tight and hot. Richie was already on edge. Love and lust swirled inside him, making Richie half crazed with need. Bryce had to come first. It was a matter of pride. Richie tried slowing things down. Their kiss softened. Richie rocked against him. Bryce moaned. The sound vibrated through their kiss, threatening Richie's sanity. Reaching between them, Richie stroked Bryce's cock, keeping time as he pumped inside the man's ass. Bryce tore his mouth away and sucked air. Richie increased his pace. Bryce's muscles tensed. The air left Richie's lungs. He focused on the pressure tightening his balls and climbing up his dick. He was so close. Ecstasy was just out of reach. Bryce's body jerked. Hot cum filled the space between them. Spasms milked Richie's cock. With his eyes squeezed shut and his forehead pressed to Bryce's shoulder, Richie let the sensations push him over the edge. An orgasm tore through him, ripping a cry from his throat. Lights popped behind his closed lids. Rambled words escaped him, forgotten as quickly as they were spoken. Richie might've begged Bryce to take him back and confessed the love that choked him every second of the day, but he couldn't stop. No one rocked him to his core the way Bryce did.

Collapsing, Richie squashed the mess between them, uncaring. He hoped they stuck together and Bryce could never leave. Their lips brushed. The sweetness of their kiss brought tears to his eyes. Richie couldn't go back to waking up without this man who owned him in every way.

"I love you, Bry. Stay," he begged before reclaiming Bryce's mouth and stealing the man's chance to shut him down. If Bryce didn't love him anymore, Richie couldn't hear the words. If this had been nothing more than sex to Bryce, Richie's heart couldn't take knowing just yet. He needed to steal more kisses, touches, and minutes. The morning would come soon enough. It always did. If Bryce was done, he'd deal with it then.

CHAPTER 5

BRYCE DIDN'T KNOW how much time passed while he watched Richie sleep. Most people softened as they dozed. Richie never stopped looking like the devil's temptation. His slashing eyebrows and hawk-like features never relaxed. Even when he dreamed, Richie looked deadly. A small smile tugged at Bryce's lips. Richie screamed danger. If Bryce was being honest with himself, that was what had lured him in when they'd met. Richie was a bad boy with a dangerous job who loved whispering dirty suggestions in Bryce's ear. He was all the things Bryce's mother warned him about. In fact, after the first time Richie met his mother, she'd let Bryce know Richie would break his heart. She'd been more right than he cared to admit.

While holding his breath and hoping he didn't

wake Richie, Bryce dragged the sheet lower, exposing more of Richie's nude body. When they'd met, Richie had been flawless. Now, deep scars covered the man's skin. It took every ounce of Bryce's self-control not to pounce and kiss each one. He couldn't change the past or take away the pain Richie suffered, but he could give the man new memories. Bryce would've thought such extensive scarring would be a turn-off. For Bryce, Richie's body had the opposite effect on him. He burned to touch the man.

Beau scratched at the door and whined. Richie rolled to his back and threw his arm over his eyes. Bryce held his breath. When Richie went back to breathing evenly and didn't wake, Bryce eased from the bed. While moving as quietly as possible, he slipped from the bedroom, doing his best to hold Beau at bay. With the bedroom door closed between them, Bryce dressed while Beau fought him for every article of clothing.

"Jesus, Beau. Give a guy a break." By the time he was sufficiently dressed, Bryce panted from exertion. He'd forgotten how playful Beau could be. "Let's find your leash."

Bryce checked the kitchen since that was where they'd kept the leash at his house. He found it hanging on a hook by Beau's food dish. Beau lost his mind when he obviously realized they were going for a walk, making it twice as hard for Bryce to snap the leash in place.

"For every minute you fight me, that's a minute I'm striking from your outside time."

As if he understood, Beau went still and let Bryce connect the leash to his collar. Bryce kissed the dog's furry cheek before straightening. He really had missed their fur baby. Bryce missed their life.

The cool night air helped to clear his mind. In the heat of the moment, Richie had begged Bryce to take him back and confessed to still loving him. Since Richie had been mid-orgasm, Bryce doubted the man remembered doing so. But, if Richie was serious, Bryce should make Richie beg. The thing was, Bryce hadn't been completely guilt free in their destruction. Richie was right. Bryce didn't leave his degree at work. He had psychoanalyzed Richie at every turn. It was part of who Bryce was. He wanted to help and make Richie better, but that was not who Richie needed him to be. Richie was getting help. He had to if he wanted to keep his job. The man wasn't one of Bryce's patients. If Bryce wanted to make his claims true, that he'd take Richie fucked up, missing limbs, or damaged beyond all repair, then he'd have to leave work at work.

Bryce spent ten more minutes letting Beau smell everything in the neighborhood before heading back. He eyed Richie's small house as he approached. It was a quarter of the size of the one they'd shared. The one Bryce still occupied. Maybe they needed a place more like this one—where they couldn't hide from each other. Even though Bryce knew he was getting ahead of himself, he couldn't stop. Richie had fired hope to life inside him. His body still burned every place Richie touched. Together, they were explosive. Bryce had tried burying his desires since Richie left. Now, he craved. When they'd been in that restaurant, as Richie pressed against him, it had taken all of Bryce's self-control not to tease Richie beneath the table. Then, tonight, all it had taken was a kiss, and Bryce had been nude. Damn, he couldn't get back to Richie fast enough.

He didn't experience an ounce of guilt as he fed Beau just to distract him so he could slip back into the bedroom without a fight. Shame still didn't rear its head as Bryce stripped and climbed into bed. Bryce didn't feel the least bit contrite as he snaked the sheet down Richie's body and pressed his lips to Richie's hip.

"I thought you'd left," Richie said around the arm still slung across his eyes.

A chuckle escaped Bryce. Busted. "I took Beau for a walk. How long have you been awake?" Bryce licked Richie's lower abdomen, watching Richie's dick stir. Damn, he couldn't get enough.

"About twenty minutes, I guess," Richie said, sucking in a breath as Bryce's tongue found the slit in Richie's crown. He craved Richie's salty flavor. "I almost got up to look for you, but I was too scared to move. Oh, goddamn," he added as Bryce licked him from root to tip.

"Why were you scared?" Bryce asked before sucking Richie's crown between his lips.

Richie's body jerked in the sexy way that always made Bryce hard. His voice came out sounding strained, but Richie still answered. "I thought you'd left me the way I'd left you. You'll never know how much I hate myself for that. I was terrified, but I also knew I deserved it."

That was enough of that. Bryce swiped his tongue across Richie's crown one final time before crawling up the man's body and pinning him to the bed. With his weight braced on his palms, Bryce set his forehead against Richie's and held his stare. "Did you notice me trying to make love to you?"

Richie nodded, squishing their foreheads together and making Bryce smile.

Bryce reached between them, palming both their erections and stroking. "Let me know when this feels like I'm through with you." Bryce went slow, tormenting himself as much as Richie.

Despite Richie looking ready to blow, the man still wouldn't relax. "Does this mean we're back together?"

An aggravated-sounding sigh escaped Bryce. He crawled from the bed, leaving Richie behind. "I guess, since you don't want me, I'll hit the shower and play with myself."

"The fuck you say," Richie growled, snagging Bryce around the waist before he made it two steps. The world tilted on edge. Bryce found himself face down across Richie's lap with his face pressed against the mattress. Richie's palm landed across Bryce's ass hard. A drop of pre-cum dripped onto Richie's lap as a loud moan slipped past Bryce's lips. It had been so damn long. Richie smoothed his hand over the spot where Bryce's ass still stung from the blow. "That was for trying to run," Richie said, sounding turned on. He stroked Bryce's ass, moving closer to Bryce's crack with each pass. Another swipe landed hard against Bryce's ass cheek. Bryce held on to the sheet and fought not to writhe in Richie's hold. Memories overcame him. Long nights and sexy games invaded his brain. Richie knew him. He knew exactly how to make Bryce beg.

Richie's hand disappeared.

"Don't stop," Bryce begged without an ounce of pride.

"Never," Richie said, sounding deadly. His squeezed Bryce's ass cheek—hard.

Bryce bit his bottom lip hard enough he tasted blood. He needed more. Finally, Richie's fingers found Bryce's hole, probing and stretching. Bryce's cock jumped and leaked. He couldn't stop himself from humping Richie's lap, seeking some form of relief.

Richie fucked Bryce's ass with his fingers like they were his dick. "Answer my question. Are you giving me another shot?"

It was a dirty move. In his current position, there was nothing he wouldn't give Richie. Bryce thanked every deity listening he'd already decided to take Richie back. Otherwise, he might've been forced to call an end to this game. Bryce wasn't sure he was that strong. Bryce nodded.

Richie's fingers disappeared. Another smack landed on his ass. "Use your words."

"Yes," Bryce cried, unsure if he'd answered Richie's question or just screamed his pleasure. He loved the sting of Richie's palm against his ass. There was a fine line between pain and pleasure. Richie was an expert at walking that line.

"Say it again," Richie demanded, barely loud enough for Bryce to hear.

"Yes," Bryce repeated. This time, he fully understood his actions. "I'm giving you another shot."

Richie shoved his way out from beneath Bryce and dropped to his knees beside the bed. With a tug, he had Bryce braced on the edge of the mattress and his tongue inside Bryce's ass. Bryce shamelessly rode the man's tongue. The sheets were so wet beneath his leaking cock anyone else might think he'd already orgasmed. Richie sank his teeth into Bryce's ass cheek, tearing a cry from Bryce's throat. "Tell me what I really want to hear," Richie demanded, obviously intent on stealing everything from Bryce.

Bryce couldn't play dumb. Richie knew him too well. "I love you."

"Good boy," Richie said, shifting to his feet. Bryce could hear him ripping into another condom. "I'm about to fuck you, Bry, and you won't come until I say so. Understood?"

Bryce nodded. His voice no longer worked. He already knew he was in for a long night. Richie was the master of keeping him on edge. Loving Richie wasn't the only reason Bryce hadn't bothered finding someone new. It was this. No one else set him free the way Richie did. No one else knew how to love him back the way Richie did. There was no one else out there for Bryce.

CHAPTER 6

THE ACHE in Bryce's cheeks wouldn't abate. He hadn't stopped smiling like a fool all day. In his profession, that wasn't a good thing. Too many times to count, Bryce had tried rearranging his features, hoping he wouldn't give a patient the wrong idea. He needed to find his somber face and hold on to it with both hands. It hadn't happened yet.

Thankfully, Fridays were his slow days. He usually only had a few morning appointments, and then he spent the rest of the day catching up on paperwork and creating a schedule for the next week. No matter how hard he tried keeping his mind on topic, his thoughts kept drifting back to Richie's bed. By the time Richie had finally given Bryce permission to come, they'd both been exhausted. Despite having had almost no sleep, Bryce could barely contain his restless energy. Richie was five floors down. All Bryce needed to do was get on the elevator.

The phone on his desk lit. "Dr. Macrae, Agent Tuthill is here to see you."

Bryce bit his bottom lip, fighting the huge grin threatening to become permanent. "Send him in."

"Yes, sir."

Bryce took a deep breath and focused on the door. No matter how hard he tried preparing himself for the sight of Richie, he couldn't. His heart still skipped a beat when the man crossed the threshold into his office. His hair was a barely contained mess of blond locks that screamed for a brush. Bryce's gaze dropped to the man's work boots before sweeping up the man's jeans that cupped all the right places. A gold badge hung from his belt. Richie's gray t-shirt was tucked in behind it while the shirt hung loose on the other side. A thick growth of dark and light hair covered the man's jaw. The smile was new. Bryce hadn't seen much of it in the past months.

"Hey, gorgeous," Richie said, closing the door behind him.

"Hey." Even to Bryce's ears, he sounded

breathless. "What brings you by? Not that I'm complaining," Bryce tacked on as he came to his feet and accepted Richie's kiss.

Their lips lingered. Richie sucked lightly on Bryce's bottom lip before pulling away. "Damn, I needed that." He sat on the corner of Bryce's desk. Bryce reclaimed his chair. "I have an appointment with Dr. Lowe in ten minutes. So I cut out a little early and snuck up here to see you. You had to leave early this morning," Richie said. He didn't do a good job of hiding his concern.

Bryce got it. They were just getting things back on track. It still felt like the smallest thing might topple them. "I had to run home to shower and change, since I don't have any clothes at your place. I was running behind, so I drove to work today."

Richie linked his fingers through Bryce's and stared at their joined hands. "We should remedy that."

A bark of laughter escaped Bryce. "Remedy what? Me driving to work?"

Richie shook his head. He lifted his chin, meeting Bryce's gaze. "You not having any clothes at my place."

Bryce didn't know what to say. It seemed crazy

to try to go back to only dating when they'd been engaged, but Bryce wasn't sure jumping back into living together was the right choice. "Um. Well, I—"

"Don't tell me no yet," Richie said, coming to his feet and pushing Bryce's chair back. "Give me a chance to persuade you," he added, going down onto his knees. Bryce forgot the point he should've been arguing when Richie tugged at his belt. "I want my life back," Richie said, going for the zipper of Bryce's pants. "You're my life."

"Richie," Bryce said, searching for some ground to stand on with Richie intent on going down on him.

Richie smirked. "Don't worry. Not a drop of cum will stain this expensive suit."

Bryce had nothing. His dick was in Richie's hands and there was no stopping things. As always, Richie was the one in control. Bryce was just along for the ride. "Unless you don't want me," Richie teased as Bryce went hard in his hand. The thing was, if the moment had only been about Bryce getting his cock sucked, he could've pushed Richie away. It wasn't. Richie was smiling and teasing, the way he used to before Mexico. Before he'd turned into a stranger. This Richie was the one he'd fallen for. Bryce couldn't stop staring at the man on his knees.

He licked his lips, suddenly nervous he was getting too hopeful. "I want you."

While holding Bryce's gaze, Richie lowered his head. His tongue shot out and brushed Bryce's crown. Bryce's grip tightened on the arms of his chair. Richie opened his mouth and sucked Bryce past his lips. He hollowed his cheeks, making Bryce's head spin. When Richie took Bryce down his throat, a moan escaped Bryce. At the sound, Richie changed angles, bending over Bryce's lap and bobbing on his dick. Bryce tried to watch. His eyes wouldn't stay open. The pleasure was too much. Leaning his head back, Bryce let Richie please him. He found himself sliding down and lifting his hips, taking what he wanted. There were blow jobs and then there was Richie's hot mouth. No one sucked dick like Richie—like he loved it. He always ensured Bryce's cock brushed the roof of his mouth and he kept the perfect suction. In Richie's mouth, Bryce forgot everything else. He was transported back to the home they'd shared. The bed where they'd spent their nights. The days when this man never would've hurt him.

Bryce's muscles tensed. He held his breath.

Ecstasy crawled up his shaft. An explosion of breath-stealing waves of pleasure overtook him. Bryce gasped as Richie licked and sucked, refusing to let Bryce's orgasm end. Bryce held the man's head and openly fucked his mouth.

Richie pulled away and shot forward, capturing Bryce's lips. Their tongues met. The familiar flavor of Richie mixed with his own cum coated Bryce's tongue. "I love you," Richie whispered against his lips, stealing another piece of Bryce's heart.

"I love you too, baby," Bryce said, trying to drag the man closer.

"Dr. Macrae, Director White would like to see you in his office."

Bryce's head whipped around. He stared at his lit phone. Bryce had seen the director of the coalition three times in his career. The day he'd been hired, the day Richie had gone missing, and the day Richie had been rescued. He couldn't think of a single reason he'd need to see the man today. "Okay. I'm on my way up." Bryce met Richie's stare. The deep line between Richie's eyes said he was every bit as confused as Bryce. "It seems I'm going to see Director White. I guess, text me when you get done seeing Dr. Lowe."

Richie came to his feet and helped Bryce

straighten his clothes. "Sure thing." Richie's face lit. "Maybe you're getting a promotion."

"To what?" Bryce asked with a snort. There wasn't much room for advancement in his job.

"Who knows?" Richie said with a shrug. "Keep me posted." Richie captured Bryce's lips for a quick kiss before heading for the door. "Oh, and Bry," he said over his shoulder as he opened the door. "I haven't forgotten what we were discussing before we were interrupted. We'll revisit that later too."

Bryce chewed his bottom lip, trying not to give in. He already knew Richie would win this argument. Richie always won. "It's a date."

With a final wink, Richie closed the door behind him, leaving Bryce to his worries. There was never a good reason to see the director. Fuck it. He headed for the door. Bryce had already been thinking about starting his own practice. There was nothing the man could say to ruin Bryce's life. Richie and him were working through their issues. Things were okay. Whatever happened would happen. Bryce had everything he needed without this place.

Twice Richie forced Dr. Lowe to fuss at him

about looking at his phone. Richie couldn't help it. People didn't get called to Director White's office for no reason. He knew Bryce hadn't done anything wrong, but still. Richie worried. By the time his session ended, Richie burst from the man's office like he'd been held against his will. Rather than heading back for his desk, Richie made his way back to Bryce's office. The suspense was killing him.

Bryce's receptionist, Cyndi was packing up to leave for the day. She glanced up when Richie came through the door. "I'm sorry. Dr. Macrae has already left."

Richie blinked. "Left? That was fast."

Cyndi nodded and went back to gathering her things. "I'm sure he was ready to get out of here."

"Who isn't?" Richie said, trying to lighten the mood. Cyndi was never overly friendly, but she usually smiled.

"Right?" she said, sounding absent as she slung her purse over her shoulder. She met his gaze. "If you'll excuse me. I have to pick my kids up early from school today."

Richie held the door for her and let her pass. His mind raced. Why had Bryce gone home without texting him? Worry ate at his gut. As he followed Cyndi to the elevator, he pulled his phone from his back pocket and sent off a quick message to Bryce.

Richie: *Cyndi says you left. What happened?*

He chewed his bottom lip as he rode the elevator back to the twelfth floor and made his way back to his desk. His eyes wouldn't stop moving toward his phone. Bryce had driven to work. It was possible he was still in the car and couldn't respond. Richie pulled up his case files on the computer and went to work. Concentration evaded him. He powered through another hour before checking his phone again. Bryce still hadn't responded. Richie snatched up the phone on his desk and dialed the man's number. It went straight to voicemail.

"Call me back," Richie demanded, not bothering to temper his growing his anger. Worrying pissed him off.

After slamming the receiver down and getting some odd looks from neighboring desks, Richie minimized his work files and pulled up his employee page. He checked his vacation hours. Since he'd already been on medical leave for part of the year, he hated to leave early, but fuck it. After clearing it with his boss, Richie was out of there. The train ride was hell. He sent three more texts to Bryce. Each went unanswered. The forty-five minutes it took him to get home almost killed him. When he spotted Bryce's Audi in the driveway and Bryce sitting on the porch, Richie's relief warred with his need to leap from the moving car.

He measured each step he took in Bryce's direction, hoping to keep his temper from erupting. Richie barely kept a lid on his reactions to anything unpleasant nowadays. He tried focusing on Bryce's soft-looking blue t-shirt and blue jeans. Fuck. Bryce was the sexiest man on the planet. Richie just hoped he still belonged to him. "I've been texting and calling," Richie said the minute he was within earshot.

Bryce nodded. "I saw."

Richie's jaw popped. He wondered if he'd crack a tooth. "And chose to ignore me, I see."

Bryce's chest expanded as he took a deep breath. It sounded ragged and set Richie's already frayed nerves on edge. Bryce motioned toward an overnight bag at his feet. "I brought clothes." He smiled, but the gesture looked strained.

Richie knew Bryce too well. Something was up. "That makes my day, baby. What's wrong?"

"Nothing," Bryce said, shaking his head. "After I left work, I was on my way home, trying to decide what to do with my life now that I'm unemployed.

The only thing I could think about was how much I want to be here with you, and Beau, of course."

His knees weakened. Richie sat on the steps. "They fired you?"

Bryce shook his head. "I quit."

"Would you like to tell me why or do you plan to make me drag every detail from you?" Richie carefully pronounced each word, because he needed Bryce to know he was in his corner. Always.

Bryce leaned forward and set his forearms on the porch railing before leaning his chin on his arms. He held Richie's stare. "They made me choose. My job or you. I chose you."

Disbelief warred with rage. Despite their six-month separation, they'd been together almost three years, and they'd worked at the same place the entire time. Richie didn't understand why it would be a problem now. "What?"

"It seems, when you came back from medical leave and got set up with our psych team, you became off-limits to me. If I wanted to continue working for the coalition, I couldn't continue seeing you."

Richie blinked. His disbelief deepened. "And you chose me over your job, even though I left you and fucked up your life? Why would you do that?"

A heartbreaking smile touched Bryce's lips. "I told you, I'd take you any way I could get you. This is part of it. I'd rather be with you, and be happy, than anywhere else in the world. Besides," Bryce said, straightening. "I'd already decided to go into private practice before they forced me out."

Richie turned away and stared at the mailbox. It was the safest place for him to look. The last thing he wanted was for Bryce to see the anger in him and think it was directed his way. He'd given fifteen years and his sanity to the DEA. Now he sat behind a desk, doing a job he hated for those people —bosses who would let someone like Bryce get away. A department that tried coming between Bryce and him right when they'd finally found a way back to each other.

"Do you think you'll need some security at this new practice?"

Bryce moved from the chair to the step. His thigh touched Richie's. Richie couldn't resist taking his hand. "You love the DEA. I left. There's no need for you to leave too."

Richie looked over, meeting Bryce's gaze. He needed Bryce to see the truth in his eyes. "I hate it there. Since I came back, it's not the same. People look at me like I might fall apart at any second. I'm working a pity job, because they don't feel they can fire me after everything I gave for them. But, baby, I fucking hate it."

Bryce brushed his thumb over Richie's knuckles. For once, the understanding in the man's gaze didn't look like pity or like he had brought his degree home. Bryce genuinely seemed to understand. "I hated it too."

A bark of laughter escaped Richie at Bryce's confession. "Why have you stayed? You could've worked anywhere."

The sweetest smile Richie had ever seen touched Bryce's lips. "There's this sexy guy who stares at me every day on the train. I worried, if I quit, I'd miss my chance of seeing him work up the nerve to talk to me."

"What's he look like? I'll beat his ass." Bryce's laughter was everything. He made Richie want happiness and light back in his life. He wrapped his arm around Bryce's waist and tucked the man against his side. "Better yet, I'll spank yours."

"It's not good business to threaten your boss."

A jolt of excitement hit Richie in the chest. "Are you being serious?"

Bryce flashed him a bright smile. "If you're up for the challenge, I have a few thoughts."

"I'm up for anything." Richie didn't bother hiding the innuendo in his tone.

The hand on Richie's thigh crept higher. "How do you feel about me selling my house, moving in here, and using the money from the sale to set up the practice? I have quite a bit saved, but if we're both depending on this, then we'll need all the cushion we can get."

The amount of faith Bryce showed him, considering all the mistakes Richie had made, was humbling. "I'm with you all the way, baby. For tonight, though, I think we should go inside and you should let me tie you to the bed."

Bryce sucked in an audible breath. "Damn, I love you."

Richie didn't rush inside. Instead, he held tighter to Bryce. "I love you too." He pressed his lips to Bryce's forehead, letting his anticipation grow. Not only did Richie look forward to ushering Bryce inside where they could play for hours, Richie couldn't wait to pick up where they'd left off. He'd once promised Bryce the world. Now it was time to make good on his word. Bryce was the love of his life. Losing him had been his biggest nightmare come true. Richie fully intended to spend the rest of his years giving Bryce a happy life.

CHAPTER 7

RICHIE COULDN'T LIE. He was nervous as hell. It wasn't the first gathering with all his friends since he'd come home. In fact, they'd met at Wyatt's mom Ella's house for Benny's birthday party not that long ago. The problem was that Richie didn't feel comfortable with anyone other than Bryce any longer. These people were family. He couldn't stop trying. Richie already knew what that path led to, and he never wanted to go there again. Plus, he'd enlisted his friends' help. They never let him down. He just hoped he made it through the day without puking.

Ella fussed with Richie's shirt. "How are you getting Bryce here without him suspecting anything?"

"Jayden," Richie said, trying not to chew a hole through the inside of his cheek. "He asked Bryce to lunch. He's kept him trapped most of the day, and then he's bringing Bryce here, telling him he needs to pay a speeding ticket."

"Smart," Ella said, sounding absent. "Now that I'm seeing you in this light, I don't like this shirt. Take it off. Let's try the pink one instead." Richie unbuttoned his shirt. He didn't have time to argue. Bryce would be there any minute and he didn't want to get caught shirtless. Wyatt and Darrel had pulled some strings, securing the private room inside the courthouse. With Ella's help, they'd gotten everything decorated in record time. Richie needed this to be perfect. He peeled off his shirt. The room fell silent.

Richie glanced around. Everyone was staring at him. "What?" At his question, Darrel, Benny, and Wyatt went back to chatting with their friend Zack, who was a priest of some sort, as if nothing happened. It hit Richie. They hadn't known. Bryce always looked at Richie like he was the sexiest man on the planet. Despite the awkwardness of the moment, a smile tugged at Richie's lips. He was making the right decision. His time in Mexico had left his body a mess of ugly scarring. Sometimes, he caught sight of himself in the mirror and it would strike him how different he looked. But he'd never felt it, because of Bryce. Richie knew, when Bryce looked at him, he didn't see a single imperfection.

Ella cleared her throat and glanced away. She handed him the pink shirt. As Richie pulled it on, Ella swiped at her eyes and cleared her throat again. "It breaks my heart," she said, making an awkward moment even more uncomfortable, but Richie got it. He understood he wasn't the only one affected by his ordeal. "I was so scared when you disappeared. It doesn't seem like there's ever a good time to say I love you. You boys are not my sons, but you are to me. Don't scare me like that again."

Richie bit back a smile. "Yes, ma'am, and I love you too."

The door opened behind them. Richie spotted Bryce and Jayden. Bryce was focused on Jayden, speaking in low tones. Richie recognized the moment it dawned on Bryce they weren't there for Jayden to pay a ticket. His gaze moved over the room, landing on the flowers and each person before he finally met Richie's stare. He moved in Richie's direction. A deep line appeared between his brows. Richie met him halfway.

"What's going—"

Richie dropped to one knee, cutting off Bryce's question. Before that moment, he'd been more than nervous. In truth, he'd been fucking terrified. Now that Bryce was there, staring down at him, everything felt right again. "I know you've told me yes once already, but that was before, and you deserve a second chance to tell me no. Will you marry me?"

Bryce's eyebrows rose. He didn't look elated. Some of Richie's confidence fled. "I'm confused. You're asking me to marry you in a courthouse? I meant it when I said yes the first time."

Richie couldn't stop smiling. "I'm asking you to marry me today. With our friends as witnesses."

Bryce's lips twitched, as if he fought his smile. He bent and touched his lips to Richie's ear, keeping his answer for Richie alone. "I'd marry you in a shit house with only a hoodoo priest as our witness. This is better, but as much as I love seeing you on your knees, I don't like other people seeing you on them."

"I love you," Richie said before he could stop himself.

Bryce caressed his jaw, still brushing the shell of Richie's ear with every syllable he spoke, and making it harder for Richie to stand. "I love you too. You look sexy in pink."

"For fuck's sake," Ella called, interrupting him. "What did he say? Are we having a wedding today or not?"

"I said yes," Bryce said, pulling Richie to his feet. "But," he added, cutting through the happy chatter that smattered the room. "We have a couple of details to work out. Please, give us a minute."

Richie cast a glance around the room as Bryce dragged him toward a nearby door. Wyatt stood leaned against a table with Benny standing between his legs and leaned against the man's chest. Ella looked as if she wasn't sure what to think while Darrel spoke to an unresponsive Jayden, who wouldn't even look the man's way. Everyone seemed willing to wait until Bryce dealt with whatever he needed. Richie couldn't think about it. Bryce had agreed to marry him. He would tackle anything else Bryce threw his way as it came.

Bryce opened the door. It was a walk-in closet that seemed to be used to keep coats and boxes of copier papers. "This'll work," Bryce said, flipping on the light. "Don't go anywhere," Bryce said to the room at large as he tugged Richie inside and closed the door behind them. As Richie looked on, Bryce took off his suit jacket and draped it over a box. He sat and pointed at the spot between his feet. "You, stand here."

Richie did as bade, moving to stand between Bryce's feet. "What do we need to iron out?"

Bryce smirked. "They say, once you're married, you can kiss blow jobs goodbye," Bryce said as he worked the buttons loose on Richie's shirt.

A snort escaped Richie. "I doubt that's true of us."

Bryce shrugged. "Still, you'd better not risk it." His gaze ate up the sight of Richie, making Richie burn. "Goddamn," Bryce breathed, sounding turned on. He ran his hands up Richie's bare chest before swiping downward and going to work on Richie's pants. "You're so beautiful, you leave me speechless."

Richie stared down at Bryce. He was the one without words. In a matter of seconds, inside a dingy closet, Bryce had him hot as hell and ready to beg for Bryce's mouth. As Bryce set his erection free, he met Richie's stare. Richie forgot to breathe. That was all he forgot. He was hyper aware of every other detail of the moment. Bryce believed he was beautiful. It wasn't just words. The truth was in the man's eyes. They were in a tiny closet. He should be freaking out. Instead, he couldn't focus on a thing beyond Bryce. As Richie looked on, Bryce lowered his chin and tongued Richie's crown. Richie locked his knees as they weakened. His hand lifted without thought. He stroked Bryce's jaw as the man swallowed his cock. A gasp escaped Richie. He already knew he wouldn't last long. Bryce was too talented. The man left no doubt he loved sucking Richie's dick and that shit was intoxicating as hell. Bryce set a pace that had Richie riding his lips with no control over the rolling of his hips. He needed the growing pleasure that was just out of his reach.

"I love you," Richie chanted. "You're everything to me."

Bryce took him deep at just the right angle at the perfect time. A wave of ecstasy overcame Richie, stealing his orgasm. He covered his mouth, hoping to smother his cries as Bryce sucked, swallowing the evidence while stealing every aftershock he could. He concentrated on breathing as Bryce came to his feet. He kissed a path up Richie's body while straightening his clothes. Their lips met. Love rocked Richie to his core. In his head, he made Bryce all the promises as they kissed. He would make this man happy. Every day. For the rest of their lives. Nothing would ever tear them apart.

———————

WHILE STARING at Benny's perfect skin tone and ignoring Darrel's stare, Jayden listened to Benny's story. Those were always great.

"So, there I was—stuck in the bathroom with nothing but an old, flimsy fly swatter and this giant lizard. I was swatting it. It was running in circles—unfazed and making no attempt to leave. I thought, great. This damn lizard likes getting spanked. I've found the only BDSM lizard in the world, and I'll never get out of here."

Jayden envied Benny. The man was smart, good-looking, funny, and everyone always hung on his every word. Even the dude wearing a priest's collar couldn't stop staring. The guy's voice gave away his eagerness to know more.

"Why didn't you step on it?"

Benny looked incredulous. Jayden bit back a laugh. "Are you fucking kidding me? I was barefoot."

Jayden lost the battle against his laughter as Benny cursed at a priest.

"Jayden."

At the sound of his name falling from Darrel's lips, Jayden's hand automatically went to his stomach. Why did Darrel always make him weak? The closet door opened, sparing Jayden from having to respond. Instead, he watched Bryce and moved to stand at the man's side. Every time he looked at Bryce, pride and love swelled in his chest. No one else had ever been there for him in every way the way Bryce had. No one could ever know how far Bryce had gone to keep Jayden sane. That was why, as he stood at Bryce's back and watched the man marry the only person he'd ever love, Jayden made his decision. He'd been the last one to join their group of friends. Benny didn't count since he was Wyatt's husband. Since he'd been the last to join, Jayden would be the first to leave. It was only fair. Plus, he couldn't stay. Too much had come to pass. With the constant wildfires in California, they were always in need of emergency personnel. He'd been thinking about it for a while. It was time for him to go.

As Bryce repeated his vows, Jayden glanced over and met Darrel's gaze. He'd been such a fool for thinking the man could ever love him. Darrel didn't love anyone but himself. Yeah, it was time for him to make his move to Cali, and let Bryce have his happily-ever-after. Jayden hadn't been meant for happiness. If he stayed, he never would be.

KEEP an eye out for Jayden's story, *His Salvation.*

Bryce and Richie play a large role in Jayden's book. You'll get an update on their new start and Bryce's new business venture.

Charity Parkerson is an award winning and multi-published author with several companies. Born with no filter from her brain to her mouth, she decided to take this odd quirk and insert it in her characters.

*Seven-time Readers' Favorite Award Winner
    *2015 Passionate Plume Award Finalist
    *2013 Reviewers' Choice Award Winner
    *2012 ARRA Finalist for Favorite Paranormal Romance
    *Five-time winner of The Mistress of the Darkpath

Connect with her online:

--Join my street team: facebook.com/TeamCharityParkerson
    --Sign up for my newsletter: http://bit.ly/CharityNews
    --Website: charityparkerson.com

--Facebook:

facebook.com/authorCharityParkerson

facebook.com/TheMenofSin

--Twitter: twitter.com/CharityParkerso

admin@charityparkerson.com

www.ingramcontent.com/pod-product-compliance
Lightning Source LLC
Chambersburg PA
CBHW070941250626
47159CB00009B/3339